INTIMATE CONFESSION

"Will you please stop milording me?" Lord John remembered that Phillida was not up to snuff. If he were to get their friendship on a more informal basis, he would simply have to ask that it be so. Besides, it was more and more difficult to remember to call her Miss Morgan when he always thought of her as Philly. He glanced at her and nearly chuckled at her shocked expression. "We've become friends, have we not?" he coaxed. "Such good friends that perhaps we might begin to use each other's name?"

Phillida hesitated. "Certainly we may—when alone, my lord, but I fear it might mislead people into thinking we've a decided partiality for each other if it were known by others that we do so."

"But we do have a decided partiality. At least, I do . . . Phillida."

Instantly her heartbeat increased unbearably. Her hands gripped each other tightly, but she gave no other sign of the sudden discovery that she'd done a most unwise thing: Phillida Morgan, spinster, had fallen in love with a rogue . . .

Books by Jeanne Savery

The Widow and the Rake
A Reformed Rake
A Christmas Treasure
A Lady's Deception
Cupid's Challenge
Lady Stephanie
A Timeless Love
A Lady's Lesson
Lord Galveston and the Ghost
A Lady's Proposal
The Widowed Miss Mordaunt
A Love for Lydia
Taming Lord Renwick
Lady Serena's Surrender
The Christmas Gift
The Perfect Husband
A Perfect Match
Smuggler's Heart
Miss Seldon's Suitors
An Independent Lady
The Family Matchmaker
The Reluctant Rake
An Acceptable Arrangement

Published by Zebra Books

An Acceptable Arrangement

Jeanne Savery

ZEBRA BOOKS
Kensington Publishing Corp.
http://www.kensingtonbooks.com

ZEBRA BOOKS are published by

Kensington Publishing Corp.
850 Third Avenue
New York, NY 10022

The poem on page 7 is from *The Complete Poetical and Dramatic Works of Sir Walter Scott,* With an Introductory Memoir by William B. Scott. George Routledge and Sons, Broadway, Ludgate Hill, London, 1887, p. 528.

All Kensington titles, imprints and distributed lines are available at special quantity discounts for bulk purchases for sales promotion, premiums, fund-raising, educational or institutional use.

Special book excerpts or customized printings can also be created to fit specific needs. For details, write or phone the office of the Kensington Special Sales Manager: Kensington Publishing Corp., 850 Third Avenue, New York, NY 10022. Attn. Special Sales Department. Phone: 1-800-221-2647.

Zebra and the Z logo Reg. U.S. Pat. & TM Off.

First Printing: January 2004
10 9 8 7 6 5 4 3 2 1

Printed in the United States of America

To Gene
Who should'a growed up to be an editor.
Thank you, Friend.
and
To Esther
who grew up to be an agent.
Thank you, Friend.

My Aunt Margaret's Mirror

There are times
When Fancy plays her gambols, in despite
Even of our watchful senses, when in sooth
Substance seems shadow, shadow substance seems,
When the broad, palpable, and marked partition,
'Twixt that which is and is not, seems dissolved,
As if the mental eye gain'd power to gaze
Beyond the limits of the existing world.
Such hours of shadowy dreams I better love
Than all the gross realities of like.

—Anonymous

One

Tuttles, his broad brow topped by a mane of white hair of which he was secretly proud, walked in his usual stately manner into Lord John's bedroom. He bowed. "Your lordship rang?" He heard his master out and—the perfect butler—didn't so much as blink at the odd request made by this man he'd known from birth. "Yes, m'lord. Are there restrictions, m'lord, on the sort of wife I'm to find you?"

"Restrictions, Tutt?" asked Lord John with airy nonchalance.

"Yes m'lord. Must she be yellow-headed, f'instance, or a recognized diamond? Or perhaps she must be well-dowered?"

"No restrictions, Tutt." Lord John tipped back his head and set the heavily starched layers of his cravat just so before slowly lowering his chin. He stared at his reflection, studying the creases produced by this simple maneuver. "That'll do," he said. "Now, Tuttles, about this wife. Not platter-faced, I think. Couldn't do my duty by a platter-faced old witch, so not too *ugly* and not *too* old. Hair color is not a consideration. And no need to be greedy, is there, so the size of her dowry needn't concern us." Lord John chose a fob with great, if unusual, deliberation. He glanced up, meeting his butler's bland gaze. "Perhaps, Tutt, the name requires she be of good family?" he suggested to the man who, while still a footman, had been, in the years of his fatherless innocence, both confidant and conspirator.

"Yes, m'lord. Not a cit nor too near the stink of the shop—is granddaughter too near, m'lord?"

"For myself, you understand, I'd not care, but the *name*, Tutt"—Lord John's brows rose—"not to mention my mother, of course, requires that I pretend to be uppish."

Thinking, as was his master, of Lady John's crochets, Tuttles agreed the *name* was important. "Great-granddaughter at a minimum, then."

"And, Tuttles, not too young. The young," said Lord John with a well-simulated shudder, "giggle."

"No giggles, m'lord," said Tuttles solemnly. "I'll remember that."

Abandoning the affected pose he'd adopted for this conversation, the aristocratic nose of Lucas Strathedene, Lord John, Fourth Earl John and Baron Strathe, returned to a level more in keeping with nature's design and a lopsided grin appeared. It was an appealing look and he would have been shocked to learn how it tore at the hearts of young ladies and made servants swear they'd go through hell if their master asked it of them— to say nothing of soldiers who had, under his command, traversed that very place.

"Tuttles," said Lord John, ruefully, "you're not required to approach the lady once you find her. I must do that, of course." He pulled the facade of featherheaded dandy around him like a cloak. "A bore," he drawled, "but what will you? Wouldn't wish to be backward in any attention. Must treat the lady just so."

"Yes, m'lord." Tuttles maintained his rigid mien, which had never, to Lord John's knowledge, slipped— even when removing a frog which, somehow, had managed an appearance in his mother's drawing room or when consoling a small boy who had just been told he was being sent away to school.

"And, Tuttles, I've decided I'll marry by the end of the Season, which leaves us little enough time for foolin' around. Can't just pop the question and marry out of hand. Must do the pretty and meet the parents and aunts and uncles and all the family skeletons." He sighed. "So, Tutt, if you could find this paragon by the end of the month?"

"Within two weeks, m'lord?"

Lord John considered and said, "Perhaps . . . three?"

Tuttles drew in a deep breath and came near to losing his fabled sangfroid. "It isn't quite like a stroll down Bond Street to choose a dozen new handkerchiefs, m'lord."

"No it isn't, is it? Too bad one can't do just that. How nice to order her up as one does one's coats. Pick the pattern and the buttons and pay special attention to the material—only the best superfine would do, Tutt." Lord John's grin appeared, his eyes bright with laughter, but he sobered soon enough. "I suppose," he continued, "you'll find it necessary to gossip with the other but-lerin' souls at the Running Footman. Maybe buy them a glass or two? Get them talking about the young ladies in their households?" He found a handful of coins and handed them over. "Sorry to put you to the bother, Tutt."

"Oh no, m'lord. Quite all right, m'lord."

"Tuttles, one last thing about this bride of mine . . . ," said his lordship, a pensive note drawing his brows close. "I feel certain it would suit if she were a docile wife. Willing to do her duty, you know, but remaining in the background otherwise—that should upset my life to the least degree, I think. And one more small detail. See that no hint of our activities reach m'mother's ears—at least, until it's too late for her to interfere! I'll not have the lady embarrassed by Mother's manipulations."

Peer's gaze met servant's, not master and man, but two men, one commiserating with the other. Lord John turned to his bed and lifted the waistcoat. Tuttles moved to help him into it and then into his coat. "That will be all, Tutt." Tuttles quietly closed the door behind himself. *Good,* thought Lord John, *that bit of business is off and running.*

Lord John inspected his coat sleeve and sighed at the wrinkles. He was between valets at the moment. The suspicion his last man took bribes must have been justified, since he no longer ran up against one of the more persistent of the matchmaking mothers at every turn. The old harridan had managed to be everywhere he went—except his clubs. It was a wonder the woman hadn't found a way to thrust her pug-faced daughter into the gaming room at White's!

The belief that his valet had been suborned was the last straw in Lord John's battle with the husband-hunting coterie. It was time to put himself out of their way. Besides, in the two years since he'd turned thirty, the notion of taking a wife had become rooted. On that particular anniversary of his natal day, however, he'd been occupied with tracking Napoleon's Peninsular troops and was precluded from making the more delightful search for a suitable bride.

Home at last, he'd made a preliminary survey. One look over the field and he'd fallen into the mopes. Was it *possible* to find a woman he could tolerate for the rest of his life? He wasn't so discouraged, however, as to give it up and take just *any* lady to wife—especially not one of his mother's choosing. What he wanted was a peaceful life with a comfortable wife. Surely there were sensible unmarried women to be found. After all, over the years, he'd met *several* married women he thought perfectly rational and they must have been the unmarried sort at some point. Therefore it was logical to believe such must exist. Somewhere.

Thus it was that Lord John hit upon the notion of asking Tuttles to sift through the rough stones offered up on the marriage mart. His butler could search out the uncut diamonds hidden amongst them and come up with a list of three or four. He'd choose one and, after a nice uncomplicated courtship, come to an acceptable arrangement and settle down to forget that he'd had to sell out at the end of 1810, had missed this spring's offensive, hadn't been at Badajoz or the battle of Fuentes de Onoro, or Albuera—hadn't been there to help, had, by going home, failed friends who died . . . all too many friends . . . Guilt was a terrible thing, he thought.

Some minutes later, in the breakfast room, the grim expression and dark look in Lord John's eyes warned the footman, Bobs, that his master had slipped into the doldrums and that it behooved everyone to walk softly until his lordship managed, once again, to put the sanguinary memories associated with the war behind him.

Lord John would have stared in disbelief if someone had told him how well his staff knew his moods. That his servants spent their free time pondering means by which they might cut short his blackest hours would have astonished him still more. He wouldn't understand why they'd waste what little free time they had thinking about his problems, especially since he believed those problems were hidden from all and sundry, that no one knew—or cared—how desperately depressed he was that he lived when so many had died, friends he might have aided, might have saved—or might have died in their place.

Across Herrick Square in another breakfast room, a musical chuckle caused the second footman, standing beside the buffet, to smile involuntarily. Warily, his eyes shifted to Lady Brookhaven. Luckily for him, the lady had her disapproving gaze fixed on the laughing face of the woman seated to her left.

"Really, Aunt Emily," said her ladyship's great-niece, wading into yet another battle with her testy relative. "Whatever gave you the notion I require a Season? A rare bumble-broth *that* would be at *my* age! Mother and I assured ourselves your kind invitation meant you wished for younger legs to run your errands and younger eyes to do your reading. Now, in *that* capacity, I think we'd suit very well. But as a sweet young innocent on the marriage mart?" Miss Phillida Morgan grinned. "Oh, Aunt Em, you can't have thought!"

"You are barely twenty-four, m'gel, and although no one could say you're a diamond . . ."

"No one would have said that when I was in my prime." Phillida bit her lip in an attempt to control her mirth. Nothing helped. Once again her delightful contralto chuckle filled the room. This time the footman managed to restrain his nearly involuntary response and remain wooden, as was proper.

"Don't interrupt, m'gel." Lady Brookhaven's wig—it was an improbable black today—wobbled as the old lady shook her finger at Phillida. "As I was saying, you aren't and never were a diamond. But you have something better. How lucky it is I went out of my way to see your mother my last visit to Cheltenham. What good sense I showed when I ignored your mother's pleas some years ago that I take a hand in bringing you out."

Phillida's back—always properly straight—stiffened into rigidity and every sign of her usual good humor fled. "My mother would not have begged you or anyone else to bring me out."

"Oh, come down off the ropes, do. I exaggerate, of course, but your mother did write and I'm not so goosish I can't read between the lines. I'm glad I ignored her," she repeated. "Then you were unformed and awkward. Now you are a mature woman, gel, and with that certain something—" Lady Brookhaven's eyes narrowed on her bemused niece. She peered at the heavy dark hair which was never quite controlled; the madonnalike face which led one to believe Phillida a demure chit . . . until one saw her twinkling blue eyes; the lush but not overly ripe figure of which the girl seemed unaware . . . "—something," repeated her ladyship, "that men like very well in a woman. Something they look for, but rarely find outside the demimonde."

"Aunt Brookhaven!" Phillida sent a partially embarrassed, totally harassed, and definitely irritated glance toward the footman, who gave her a *What can you do?* look of commiseration before returning to immobility.

Lady Brookhaven shook a gnarled finger at her greatniece. "Don't you put on missish airs with me, gel. *I* know you're more than seven. You're as aware such women exist as I am."

"I'm not outraged by mention of the sort of woman of whom I'm supposed to be in ignorance. I am shocked you believe I would do as one of them!"

"Twiddle-poop!" Lady Brookhaven glowered. Phillida's anger, rarely of long duration, dissipated at the word, and she stifled another laugh—one which, colored by embarrassment, approached a giggle. "I said no such thing," asserted the old woman when, as she believed, she'd thoroughly intimidated her great-niece.

Phillida regained a prim mien. "Now, Aunt," she coaxed, "I'm not deaf and I distinctly heard you. I have *something* found mostly in the muslin company! You said that!"

"So I did. Didn't say you should behave like one."

"Thank goodness for small favors."

Lady Brookhaven ignored that piece of impertinence.

"However, you do have that . . . that . . . whatever it is. Now don't get angry. No one said it was a bad thing." Phillida frowned. "Gel," insisted her exasperated aunt, "I merely mean you aren't afraid of owning to the fact you have a body."

Phillida cast a quick glance down her length and blinked. Didn't everyone own a body?

"Observe the young women at Lady Gavinthorpe's tonight," continued her long-suffering relative, who was unused to explaining herself. "All those prudish misses in virginal white—tell me how they expect to hold a man."

"Aunt, I've no desire to change my unmarried state. I will happily take advantage of the Season's delights when you wish to give me a treat, but I will *not* be pushed forward like a not particularly fine import of tea the East India Company wishes to auction off to the highest bidder—but with little hope of making much of a profit," she added under her breath.

"Not tea. Ridiculous notion." Lady Brookhaven's shocked expression turned thoughtful. "Wine, perhaps. Wine improves when aged properly." Lady Brookhaven nodded, again endangering the wig's position on her shaved head. "Bubbly wine. From Champagne," she added, eyeing her niece who was, manfully, attempting to curb more laughter. "You have character. You ain't ignorant. You've the maidenly virtues and the added fillip of a sense of humor. You'll pay for dressing—even that old gown can't hide that you're properly endowed. . . . I expect little difficulty in firing you off." *Especially,* thought her ladyship, *when I've the groom in hand, another twiddle-poop if there ever was one, and much in need of a bride—although he don't know it yet.*

Phillida made a face at the suggestion she was physically well endowed. "I do wish you wouldn't continually put me to the blush, Aunt."

Lady Brookhaven's brow lowered in a way which would have warned her servants she was rapidly losing her irascible temper. "I wish *you'd* not gammon me. You haven't a notion of what I speak." Her ladyship's glower, which should have had her niece cowering—but never did—was firmly in place.

"How can I convince you I did not come to London to look for a husband?"

"You're a fool," blustered Lady Brookhaven, searching her mind for arguments against her too self-possessed niece's attitude.

Phillida, hoping to end the conversation, said, "So tell this fool what she may do for you this morning, Aunt, other than the bouquets, of course." She folded her napkin and rose to her feet.

Taking over that job had been Phillida's first effort at easing life for her aunt. Her arrangements were so artistic that Lady Brookhaven had forborne to give her best lecture concerning encroaching relatives and their well-deserved place in hell, reversing her intention entirely, and ordering her niece to do the flowers every day.

"You may think over what I've said. I'll be in the back parlor if callers come, not that any will. Now, if you'd been less reluctant to be introduced when I took you driving," she added on a sly note, "I don't doubt a number of beaux would be at the door. I don't understand you, m'gel. You should take advantage of these months in London. If not for your own sake," she added on a sudden inspiration, "then for your mother's."

Phillida, her hand on the doorknob, frowned. "My mother's sake?"

Lady Brookhaven nodded vigorously, absently catching and resetting the wig, which had slid over her forehead. She smiled beatifically: at last she had found an argument to bring her recalcitrant niece to her knees. "How blind the young are."

"Don't make mysteries, please, Aunt. How have I been blind?"

"Sir Clifford, of course."

"But what about Sir Clifford? He was my father's best friend, and . . ." Phillida's eyes widened. "You can't mean they wish to wed and will not because I'm on Mama's hands!"

Lady Brookhaven winked. "Knew you had something besides feathers in your cockloft."

"You assume they've no desire to set up a household in which a spinster daughter is permanently installed?" Phillida denied it. Sir Clifford *would* welcome her into his home. "Lady Brookhaven, I've just discovered you are not unwilling to prevaricate to get your own way," she scolded.

"Lie? *Never.*" The old lady grinned, showing more gum than was pleasant. "Believe me, gel, I *don't* lie. I may, however, stretch the exact truth a trifle—in a good cause. You, m'dear niece, are a very good cause indeed." *Or will be once I've taught you your place* was her silent caveat.

Phillida ignored the compliment. "Since you are not cutting the notion out of whole cloth, you must believe they wish to wed?" Her aunt nodded. "I don't understand, in that case, why they have not."

"Do you not?" The rhetorical question gave Lady Brookhaven time to think. Hastily she put her devious mind to work and, just in time, came up with another notion. "How do you feel about your father?" she asked.

"He was a saint," said Phillida promptly.

"Hmmm. And how do you think Sir Clifford feels about stepping into such a man's boots?"

"He has very good boots of his own," said Phillida.

"But he doesn't know you feel that way, does he? He will not usurp your father's place, m'dear."

"How silly of them. I must write Mother at once."

"*No you will not* . . . do nothing so tactless, m'gel," finished her ladyship when Phillida looked startled by the abrupt order.

"There is nothing tactless about an honest expression of my views."

Again Lady Brookhaven thought quickly. "That's not true when the parties involved believe they've pulled the wool over your eyes and will be upset to discover they have not," she said triumphantly.

"*That* problem is easily solved," said Phillida pertly. "I merely need inform Mother where I gained my information, needn't I?" Phillida whisked herself out the door before Lady Brookhaven could decide whether to scold or be amused.

Sequestered in her room, Phillida paced. It was one thing to encourage her mother to remarry without hesitation, but, however much she'd denied it to her well-meaning aunt, it would require tact to tell one's mother she had a daughter's permission to do so! Worse, there was, just possibly, something in Lady Brookhaven's view that Sir Clifford would find a grown stepdaughter who idolized her late father something of a burden.

Perhaps Lady Brookhaven, bless the old witch's ivory dentures, was correct? Perhaps she should reconsider the decision she'd made to remain a spinster—a decision made when she received an unexpected competence, an inheritance from her grandmother, which made it possible to remain unwed without becoming a burden on some wealthier relative?

Why, wondered Phillida, had she originally decided to remain single? At bottom, of course, was the impossibility of finding a man to match her father. Phillida tipped her head, thinking of the life they'd led before Mr. Morgan succumbed to a putrid sore throat. Now she was older and aware of a wider world, did she really *want* a man with her father's nature? *Could* she find

contentment in the scholarly life, her only amusement
such odd souls as those her father invited into their
home? Did that life still appeal?

Phillida admitted it did not. But, if she'd be unhappy
with that sort of marriage, neither could she abide one
of the man-milliners about whom Lady Brookhaven had
been so scathing—the prancing, sauntering popinjays.
That would never do. It was something of a problem,
then, the fact that such fops seemed to be in the major-
ity among the men she'd so far seen.

There'd been one who was different. The rider's magnificent gray gelding had taken exception to a yapping
lapdog which had tried to escape her mistress by scrab-
bling up the back of the lady's landau. The horse had
required a strong hand to bring him under control. Before
the incident, Phillida had considered the rider only a trifle less affected than the other men in the park. During the
confrontation between horse and man, however, the gentleman's expression lost its cold, bored look and took on
an animation indicative of a totally different character.

Phillida had noted the phenomenon before, a person-
ality hidden behind a facade presented to the world.
Now she admitted to curiosity and wondered how she
might meet the owner of the gray for the purpose of determining if there was a *real* man under a coat not *quite*
so tight as others wore—certainly not padded here and
pinched in there. In fact, he was the only man she'd so
far seen in London to interest her at all. In hopes of
gaining information without raising her aunt's curiosity,
she'd pointed out the gray, saying it was the best piece
of horseflesh she'd seen that day.

"Aye, the new earl always has good mounts." Then the
old woman had cackled that rather nasty chuckle Phillida was learning to dread. "Yes, a good eye for a mount,
Lucas Strathedene—Lord John, that is—whether the
four-legged kind or having only two. He's currently got

a long-legged blond, a filly with sleepy eyes, in keeping. Very like his last mistress, in fact. Lord John is nothing if not consistent."

Phillida had found no humor in her aunt's caustic comment—which surprised her. Usually she could find something at which to laugh in any situation. Now she thought of it, why did she object to the notion Lord John had an expensive Cyprian in keeping? A long-legged *blond* Cyprian? Not one to waste time on unanswerable questions, she gave it up and rang for her maid.

Lady Brookhaven had been shocked to discover Phillida had never had a lady's maid and insisted one be hired. They'd interviewed a dozen before Lady Brookhaven, bored with it all, allowed Phillida her choice.

"You rang, miss?" asked Flint.

Phillida wore a quizzical expression which made her eyes twinkle and heightened her color, if she'd only known it, besides bringing out *both* of her dimples in all their glory. "Flint, can I, as I believe I may, trust you?"

The abigail, although not long in Miss Morgan's service, had already developed a deep liking for her. She smiled at her mistress's newest start. "Trust me, miss? I certainly hope so!"

"Then, if I ask a service of you and that you not reveal it by hint or deed, you could be relied upon? I do not mean to insult you, Flint," added Phillida, although her maid showed no sign of pokering up. "I must be certain, because I would be distressed if word of what I wish were to become the latest on dit. And I believe Lady Brookhaven would be so angry, *justly* angry, she'd never speak to me again."

Flint's expression was as kind as ever, and in her eyes was that intelligent questioning look which Phillida had liked from the first moment of introduction. "I'll gladly undertake to help, miss. I'll have no difficulty keeping it under my bonnet, either."

"I thought not. You are not, I believe, a gabble-grinder—as my nurse would have said. Now, what I wish, you see, is that you discover the names of several men whom I may consider for the role of husband."

Flint hadn't known what to expect, but this was far and away from any of her guesses—which had ranged from bearing love notes to an unsuitable parti to dressing miss in boy's raiment for a clandestine stroll down St. James. Momentarily the maid reverted to her beginnings: "Lawks, miss."

Phillida chuckled. "Outrageous, isn't it? But I've noticed that the ton hide their true natures behind a pose. What I wish *you* to do is to discover how they behave when the masks are off—I think their servants would know that beyond a doubt, is that not so?"

Flint pressed two fingers against her mouth for a moment in the way she had. "There was a baronet everyone thought the world of—but we who served him knew he liked inflicting pain. Now, if the sweet innocent he married had asked her maid to discover his quirks, she might have avoided a miserable life, but she only saw his smiling public face and never looked beyond it."

"That story's enough to put one off marriage altogether. I'm already ambivalent about the notion, you see." Phillida explained about her mother's inclination to rewed and continued, "Despite a desire to help my mother, I'm selfish: I'll only accept a man with whom I've a hope of living in comfort. I am lucky in that I may be as choosy as I please, and I choose to be verrry chooosy indeed!" She said the last with *such* an impish look.

"What am I to look for in particular, miss?" asked the abigail when they stopped laughing.

Phillida's lids lowered about halfway and quivered slightly, showing off an excessive length of lashes. "It is easier to say what I do *not* want. I am not greedy, Flint. A man with no more than a competence is not to be ignored for that reason alone. But if he is an inveterate gambler, he will not do."

"No gambling."

"No *excessive* gambling. From the stories my aunt relates," said Phillida in an exasperated tone, "it appears to be virtually impossible to live in the ton and *not* gamble. But our gentleman must do so only moderately," she finished more temperately.

"Yes, miss."

"I would prefer him to be neither too young nor too old."

"Under forty, then, and over thirty. Anything else, miss? Should he be a . . . a political man or . . . or an Adonis, for instance?" asked Flint next.

"I would prefer the man have interests beyond the set of his coat! Nor would I care to be leg-shackled to a truly ugly man, but better that than to a man so enamored of his own looks he'd be impossibly vain. So, very likely *not* an Adonis." Phillida paced between her window and her desk. "Now, what else is required? Such things as kindness and intelligence go without saying, I'm sure. Ah," she added, raising one finger for emphasis, "a sense of humor!"

"Yes, miss. I can see that it wouldn't do for you to marry a man with no humor in him."

Phillida's impish look returned at her maid's dry tone. "We've determined," she went on, "he need not be wealthy nor particularly handsome and have decided on his age. Oh, dear. This is more complicated than I'd expected. I wonder if we should forget the notion. I'm certain I am asking the impossible and that it cannot be accomplished."

"Oh, but it *can*, miss." Flint then bit her lip, obviously ambivalent. Phillida gave her an expectant look. "It is the custom of us dressers," she admitted, "to discuss with our friends the tonish men who will do for our ladies—not that we pass on our decisions. That would be impertinence indeed. I promise, I can discover all we wish to know with no one the wiser. No one will suspect I give you the information because it simply isn't done."

Phillida nodded. "I can think of only one other thing I'd wish to know," she said after a moment. "Will the man allow me to be *me*, or will he require I adopt a social mask. It's so hypocritical. Besides, I'm not any good at it: I *never* do well when amateur theatricals are cast and I'm required to take a part."

"That will be difficult to determine, will it not?" asked Flint, after some thought. "How does one discover what a man will require of a wife when he's never had a wife—which raises another question. Would a widower do?"

The discussion went on in this way, each new point raising further questions. Phillida was very glad indeed when it was ended, and admitted to qualms now she'd set all in motion. But it was done. She could not call back the words and, thinking on it, she didn't wish to. But she had the oddest premonition that, rather than the simple straightforward courtship for which she hoped, this matter was much more likely to become complicated beyond belief.

Phillida went on to her next problem. She wrote to her mother rapidly in a humorous vein, and the resulting letter covered the situation of her mother, Sir Clifford, and herself with all the whimsy at Phillida's command, making a joke of whatever could be joked about and, elsewhere, lovingly encouragingly her mother, thusly: ". . . so please don't be *a poor twaddling creature*, but follow your heart and under no circumstances should you act the *goosish gudgeon*. Making a piece of work of what is a very simple thing is far more foolish than . . ."

Two

The rosy-cheeked barmaid at the Running Footman winked at Tuttles as she handed him a pewter mug. He grinned his appreciation of the buxom maid and turned to scan the room. It was too early for many servants to have found their way there. Even those with a half-day would not arrive until later. It was, therefore, the best possible time to have a quiet word with his friend Porterman, who, his joints swollen with a rheumatic complaint, had been forced to retire from service at the end of the last Season. He'd found rooms above an iron-mongery not far from the public house patronized by upper servants and, living on a barely adequate pension, spent hours in the tavern's public room nursing along the one or two heavy-wets he allowed himself each day.

Today was no exception. Unfortunately, the bent old man was not alone. A woman, dressed in the fashion of a well-paid abigail, sat with straight back and feet neatly side by side. She had a familiar look, and, after a moment, Tuttles recognized his old friend's daughter. She was a bright-eyed robin of a woman, a good trustworthy soul. If his memory hadn't failed him, the widowed Mrs. Flint was back in service. Perhaps she, too, could be of help?

"Good day to you, Mr. Porterman, Mrs. Flint." Tuttles nodded and, at a gesture from his friend, lowered himself to a place on the settle. "It's good to see you again, missus."

"And you, Mr. Tuttles. Is his lordship from town that you visit the Footman at this extraordinary time of day," teased Flint, "or are you, in imitation of so many in service these degenerate days, dropping in while on the way to or from some errand?"

"Neither, missus," said Tuttles, a tiny smile growing at the perplexed look exchanged between father and daughter. "I need help. When I require aid, I come to the best I know to get it." He raised his mug to Porterman.

"What possible help could a useless old crock like myself be to an up-and-coming young whippersnapper like yourself?"

The twelve years' difference in their ages had long been a joke between them, Tuttles retaliating by calling Porterman a naggy old codger. Unhappily, the reference Porterman made to his uselessness was *not* a jape. The former butler had grown ever more morose as his retirement developed a boring, a day-after-day sameness. He tried to rally when Tuttles dropped by, but the two knew each other too well for the sham to be effective.

"It is a trifling matter of assistance with a bit of skulduggery." He glanced at Flint. "I can trust you to keep your mummer dubbed?" he asked politely. Intrigued, and therefore forbearing to pretend she didn't understand cant words which should not have been in a feminine vocabulary, Flint nodded. Assured she'd keep still about what he had to say, Tuttles explained: "It's like this. His lordship has decided to take a wife. The instant he goes looking for one, however, he'll set the ton trailing in his wake, every mama clamoring to bring her daughter to his attention. After making a preliminary reconnaissance, as he'd say himself, he concluded most young ladies currently on the hop for a husband will not do and, while he wants a wife, he wishes to avoid harassment from the impossible sort."

Porterman exchanged a look with his daughter. Her eyes twinkled, and Porterman's eyes lit up as well. The old man felt a lightening of his spirits he'd not experienced for ever so long.

"What he requires," continued Tuttles, unaware he'd roused his colleagues to mirth, "is a slightly older woman, one who will not bore him before the wedding trip has ended. He specifically asked, for instance, that the lady *not* be a giggler. There are other requirements, as you might guess, but . . ."

Mrs. Flint doubled over, her shoulders shaking, her laughter silent. Her father, however, threw back his head, the rare sound of his chortling echoing around the huge fireplace within which the settle was placed.

Tuttles's glare passed over Mrs. Flint and settled on her father. "I do not see that what I've said is worthy of quite so much hilarity."

"Get down off your high horse, Tutt," said Porterman, suppressing a few last chuckles. "It is merely the coincidence, you see."

"I do *not* see."

Flint realized that Tuttles was seriously ruffled and that his feathers must be smoothed. "It's a coincidence, to be sure, for I am on a similar quest. The lady whom I dress has come to an identical conclusion. She's remained a spinster by choice. It has been brought to her attention that her mother wishes to remarry but has not, feeling she must stay with her unwed daughter who is, now, twenty-four years of age. The daughter feels she must sacrifice her own wishes for her mother's sake. Have I made myself clear?"

"Perfectly. She, too, has requirements?"

"Oh yes. Definitely. There is nothing totty-headed

about my mistress, Mr. Tuttles. She will not accept just *any* man for a husband."

"I suppose," said Tuttles in a faintly mocking tone, "he must be titled and wealthy and Byronic in looks?"

"Nothing of the sort," responded the maid. "He need be only *reasonably* wealthy, gamble no more than moderately, and be kind and intelligent. Contrary to your expectation, Mr. Tuttles, he should *not* be an Adonis. She claims an Adonis is too likely to be vain and selfish."

"Definitely not the usual buffle-brained tonish female," said Tuttles thoughtfully. "Are you thinking what I'm thinking?"

"Yes, I am," said Flint promptly. "I've heard much of Lord John from my father, and I believe he would do very well for my mistress. His military record was distinguished, of course, but far more important to my mind, he's a good master. That reveals a man's character, does it not?"

"That he is, missus, and so it does." Tuttles's face crumpled into a mask of worry wrinkles. "We're *that* fussed about him," he confided, momentarily changing the subject. "He's not himself. Not himself at all."

"Worried?" *That* fact worried Flint, who had no intention of recommending an ailing man to her mistress or one with financial woes. That wouldn't do.

"Just since his return from Spain, you know. He only sold out because his brother died in a carriage accident, although I think it was time and more he did. But the black moods come over him and he don't eat enough to keep a climbing boy, sleeps too much, and, when the mood is on him, spends too much time alone." Tuttles shook his head.

It was rumored many returning officers relied on drink to give them surcease from memories of terrible sieges and relentless battles. Carefully, Flint phrased a question. Immediately she was reassured. Lord John had *not* fallen into the bottle. At least not recently.

"But that is by the way," said Tuttles, embarrassed he'd been so open about something he would not normally have revealed to a soul. "If we are seriously proposing to bring your mistress together with my master, we must lay plans. I don't believe I can tell my lord the very day he asks for help that I've found his ideal. He will take her in aversion, thinking it impossible I could come up with a paragon so quickly."

"I, too, must be careful. Miss Morgan has a delightful sense of humor, but she can, I've found, be stubborn when she takes a notion into her head. For instance, Lady Brookhaven wishes to give her a Season. Miss Morgan has—oh, very politely and with much jocularity—insisted she is too old for a Season and, if Lady B. wishes, she will remain in London as Lady B.'s companion, but *not* as a burnt offering on the altar of the marriage mart."

The men chuckled. Tuttles said thoughtfully, "A witty woman with a way with words. How unusual. I believe she *will* do for his lordship."

Flint bristled, her mouth primming. "It isn't a question, Mr. Tuttles, of whether she'll do for the earl. What's important is if *he'll* do for *her*."

"Now, now," said Porterman pacifically, before the partisans could come to verbal blows, "they must do for each other and, if we're agreed it's worth a try and you both believe it must be approached in a roundabout way, then I think, Mr. Tuttles, old friend, that you should hie yourself over to the bar and return with sustenance which will aid us in furthering our discussion. We wouldn't want our throats going dry from all this talk, now would we?"

"An excellent notion. Missus?" asked Tuttles politely,

not yet forgiving her for her presumption. "What is your pleasure?"

Tuttles returned with two large and one small mug, and the conspirators put their heads together. The few patrons loitering in the Running Footman grew curious as to the subject of a discussion which resulted in occasional chuckles, several groans, and not a few soft swear words—followed, of course, by apologies to Mrs. Flint. The plotters were discovering it was not easy to evolve the means whereby a pair of stubborn individuals, who had slightly contradictory requirements in what they thought they wanted in a mate, might be induced to see each other in a favorable and, preferably, romantic light.

"Then," said Tuttles finally, "we're agreed we should leave their first meeting to chance? The town is yet thin of company, so it should be soon."

"We're agreed," said Flint. "We'll just mention the names we've picked as red herrings!"

"As you guessed, Miss Phillida, it will not be the easiest thing to discover a man who fits your ideal. Mr. Diggory, however, isn't too far outside the requirements you imposed on us." Flint finished brushing the pelisse she held and looked sideways to note her mistress's response. "He's a kind man, a Quakerish gentleman, but not of the extreme sort called Plain Quakers. He spends a deal of time doing good works, but is not against a bit of jollification. He will attend the Gavinthorpe soiree this evening."

"Quakerish?" Phillida pounced on one of the traits the conspirators hoped would put her off. "I do not know much about those people, Flint."

"No, miss, nor do I, except I've heard they believe strongly in education for both men and women and do not fear to allow their women to use their minds and work at their side in their charities."

"So what is wrong with this paragon?" asked Phillida suspiciously.

Flint bit her lip. "He is a trifle older than you wished."

"A trifle?" Suspicion grew.

"Well, he has slipped into his forties, miss." Flint drew a deep breath. "Forty-eight, to be exact. But a very well-preserved man, miss," she added hurriedly. "Still slender as you'd please and losing only a little of his hair. Please do not take the man in aversion before you even see him. He will, as I said, be attending this evening's do, and you may contrive to observe him, perhaps meet and talk with him?"

"I will not judge the man before I meet him, Flint, but I hope you can find someone a great deal nearer my ideal. The Quakers are, I believe, serious souls. I doubt they'd approve my particularly odd type of humor. I'll do what I can for my mother, but not to the point of martyring myself. I fear controlling my sense of the ridiculous would be penance indeed."

"No mother would wish her daughter to be unhappy in her marriage."

Phillida chuckled. "Now there's a plumper, Flint, if I ever heard one. Weren't you telling me just the other day about matchmaking viragos who go to any length to see their daughters wed? Even to one-eyed nonagenarians? Even to setting traps for some particularly unwilling prey and baiting them with their nubile offspring?"

"You've caught me finely, miss. But your mother cannot be that breed of woman or you would, yourself, be wed." Flint eyed her mistress thoughtfully. Miss Morgan was as friendly as a puppy and thrice as trusting. Flint stifled a sigh. They must be careful to point out only decent men: Miss Morgan, a green girl despite her years, might take it into her head to marry the wrong man, and one wouldn't wish a disaster on her!

"So," said Phillida, interrupting such thoughts, "if I'm to take particular cognizance of this man named Mr. Diggory, then we must think about readying me for an evening among the ton. It is not what I expected when I agreed to come to London, but my lady-aunt has manipulated me finely. I will, of necessity, comply with her wishes, and indulge in far more socializing than I'd thought to do."

"Such a terrible harsh duty, to be sure, miss," Flint dared to tease, meeting Phillida's eyes in the mirror.

"Yes. A severe punishment," said her mistress, managing to maintain a severe expression. "I must be a dreadful sinner to deserve it."

While Phillida and Flint discussed which of the two newly delivered gowns was more suitable for an evening devoted to conversation and cards, Tuttles stood uneasily before Lord John's desk. "Yes, m'lord. As I explained, m'lord, I merely wish to report I have the work in hand. You were correct in believing we'd have difficulty discovering the paragon you seek. But two names were mentioned which were not toooo far from your requirements."

Lord John raised a skeptical eyebrow. "Yes, Tuttles? Two, you say?"

"Yes, m'lord." Tuttles drew in a deep breath and dove in. "There is Miss Eversham, whom you may have met?"

"Eversham . . . That must be Sir Henry's daughter." Lord John frowned, lifting his gaze to stab a glare at Tuttles. "The *fat* one?" he asked, a dangerous note in his voice.

Tuttles hid a smile. "Not fat, m'lord. Or, at least, not now. She has been on Lord Byron's diet for months, m'lord. I'm told she is in much better looks. Vinegar and potatoes, m'lord," he added when something further seemed required of him.

Lord John snorted. "So she's thin now, but for *how long*, Tuttles? Until she's trapped her man and no longer? No, no, Tutt. I expect better of you."

Tuttles nodded. It was the predicted reaction. "There is also a Lady Gwendolyn Troquair, only recently come to London, m'lord, and within a year or two of her thirtieth birthday. One may believe she is of an age to have left behind the tendency to giggle, m'lord."

"I have noticed age is no absolute guarantee against the condition, Tutt," said Lord John absently. His gaze pinned Tuttles. "Why," he drawled, "is this paragon still unwed at such an advanced age?"

Tuttles squirmed. "I believe, m'lord, she has very little dowry, but your lordship said that was not an obstacle."

Lord John eyed his butler. "Is that all?"

"She's rather tall, m'lord," said the butler with assumed reluctance.

"Tall, Tuttles?"

"I haven't seen the lady, m'lord." Tuttles stared over Lord John's head, since he couldn't bring himself to meet his master's eyes. "I only tell you what I gathered from conversation at the Running Footman this morning."

Lord John sighed. "An exceedingly boring morning, I'm sure. Nor can I blame *you* that the ton is lacking the sort of woman for whom I search."

"M'lord!" Tuttles nearly panicked at this sign his master was already losing faith in their project. "It's early days yet. Do give me a little more time before you assume any such thing." Lord John nodded—rather morosely, thought Tuttles. "I believe Lady Gwendolyn is to be present at the Gavinthorpes' soiree this evening, m'lord. For want of a better objective," he coaxed when his words brought no response, "you might attend? Just to lay your peepers, er, your glims, hmm, I mean your *eyes* on the lady?" he wheedled, crossing his fingers behind his back. Their plan required Lord John attend and, with any luck at all, meet Mrs. Flint's Miss Morgan.

"I am expected at White's, Tuttles, but I might drop in for a moment. Lady Gavinthorpe is m'mother's godmother, I believe, and one is forced by convention to do the pretty when the hostess has a connection of that sort with the family. And," he added with a touch of the insouciance he donned as armor, "given Lady Gavinthorpe's relationship with my mother, no one can suspect my *real* purpose in attending. Isn't that right, Tutt?"

"Yes, m'lord. I will return to the tavern this evening when there will be a larger number of associates to whom I may resort for information and will endeavor to find you a lady whom you will not take in aversion, m'lord."

"Very good, Tuttles."

Lord John leaned back in his chair, turning it slightly so he could stare into the garden behind his town house. His eyes darkened, and Tuttles stifled a wish to say "there, there," and pat his master's head as, once, he would have done. He left the library, and the footman stationed in the hall raised a questioning eyebrow. Tuttles replied with a grimace: Lord John had not yet come out of the mopes—although he'd roused during their talk, which was, thought Tuttles, a good sign. Perhaps the search for a wife would occupy his lordship's mind and shake out the nightmares dwelling there.

Phillida glanced back down the Gavinthorpes' hall, noted no one was looking, and ducked through the door to her right. She closed it and leaned back against it, heaving a tremendous sigh of pure relief.

"If you are awaiting your lover and in need of privacy, go somewhere else. This room is taken."

Phillida straightened, her closed eyes popping open. "My lo . . . ? To the contrary, sir, whoever you may be. I am attempting to escape . . ." Phillida sighed in exasperation. "There I go again, explaining myself to a total stranger. I find it an utterly unfair world," she complained. "Not only is one forbidden to speak to someone to whom one has not been introduced, but that same someone has already taken this hiding place when I need one badly. Are you remaining long?"

Lord John's lips twitched at the wide-eyed hopeful look. "I expect to remain as long as I must remain in this house." He pulled out his watch and flipped it open. "Another ten minutes should do. By then my hostess will not be too insulted when I approach her to say good-bye. I apologize if I discommode you, ma'am," he added as an afterthought, obviously not meaning it.

"It is not your problem, sir. I'll find me another hiding place."

"Why would a lovely young woman like yourself wish to hide?" asked Lord John, in hopes of amusement to fill what had become a tedious interlude.

"Lovely? *Young?*" Phillida's enticing chuckle rippled around them, one of her dimples quivering into view. "It must be true, what I've heard."

"What have you heard? Perhaps I may verify it?" said Lord John quickly. The intruder was groping behind herself for the doorknob and, finding the chatter between them surprisingly entertaining, he didn't wish her to depart. *Who the devil can she be?* he wondered.

"Why, only that candlelight tends to be kind to the aging."

It was Lord John's turn to laugh. He, too, had one of

those rather nice laughs which made one feel better just hearing it—like warm flannel on a cold day, a grandmotherly type had once said of it. "I've heard that, but what has it to do with you?"

"I am four and twenty and may be considered firmly on the shelf, my lord," she answered in a prim voice, but her dancing eyes belied her claim and, this time, dimples flirted from both her cheeks.

Had she recognized him? She was no longer calling him "sir." "If you told no one, I'm certain you could pass for barely twenty—perhaps less."

She chuckled again. "Why would I wish to do any such thing? It would be a lie, and I dislike lies of all things. *Living* one is certainly no better than *telling* one."

"Then you are not in London to join in the annual hunt for a husband?" he asked. Her gown was too rich for her to be someone's poor relation, and her manner too easy. Quite obviously she had breeding and money. *Who the devil is she?* he asked himself again.

"I decided years ago that the spinster state would suit me right down to the ground. . . ." A conscious look widened her eyes and her pretty mouth thinned. She lowered long lashes to reddening cheeks. "That is," she amended carefully, "up until recently, it suited me. I find it expedient to marry—but only if I can find a man with whom I may live a comfortable life. It won't be an easy task, I think. Oh, dear. That sounds as if I am impossible to please, does it not?"

Was she really as naive as she sounded, or was this an exceedingly unusual plot to entrap him? Though he wished a wife, Lord John did not want to be *forced* into taking one. He bent a thoughtful, considering look onto the seemingly innocent stranger who had burst so suddenly into his solitude. Instead of blushing—or, worse, giggling—she tipped her head and looked right back. He found himself smiling again.

"You've recognized me, ma'am, but I fear I cannot put a name to you."

"I *didn't* recognize you, my lord, when I first entered, because the last time I saw you, you were controlling a fractious horse and dressed for riding. You do not look anything the same." He recognized her considering look and stiffened, wondering what she was up to now. "It has occurred to me, Lord John, that you might be useful to me."

Lord John blinked. "I might be *useful?*"

"Yes." She nodded, the candlelight revealing a strand of burnished copper in the brunette locks. "In my husband hunt. I've indicated I'm rather particular?" He nodded warily. "Yes, well, I think you very likely know just the sort of man who would appeal to me. You could introduce us and stand back and see if anything happens."

A faint emotion he discovered was pique made him ask, "You do not count me among your possible choices?"

Color gave her cheeks a faint glow, but she answered steadily enough. "When I first saw you standing there by the hearth, my lord, I did. Just for a moment. But I've remembered what my aunt said, and it will not do."

"Might I ask," he said, his voice glacial, "what your aunt said of me?"

Phillida eyed him for a moment and shook her head decidedly. "No, I think you may *not* ask. Nor may I tell you. It wouldn't be at all proper."

"You worry, *now*, about the proprieties?" he said, sneering, upset but unable to say why. "We've been closeted alone for upwards of fifteen minutes. You have been compromised, my dear, or are you aware of that and only *pretending* disinterest in me as a husband?"

"How absurd you are. No one knows, so neither of us can possibly be compromised." Phillida frowned, her own temper on the rise as his insinuation was understood. "However, it would be just my luck to have an interfering and high-nosed dowager find us here and raise a dust. I certainly don't wish that, so I'll leave you to your solitude."

"Wait." He took a step toward her. "You thought I might be of use to you. Have you changed your mind?"

Phillida tipped her head. "Are you suggesting you might be willing?"

"I might," he said cautiously.

"Then, assuming you haven't come to your senses once you've slept on it, you might *accidentally* find me at Ackermann's Repository of Arts in the Strand. We could arrange a time when we might discuss my problem."

"Why not now?"

"Because I told one of those lies I detest—that I must fix a rent in my gown. If I've truly been here upwards of fifteen minutes, I must return, but if my aunt introduces me to one more bore I'll . . ." Phillida drew in a deep, steadying breath. "Why, I'll say how-do-you-do and be just as pleasant and quiet-spoken as I have for the past interminable hours. Good evening."

"Wait!" She paused. "What time tomorrow?" he asked, adding, "I will take you up in my curricle. That should give us privacy for our plotting."

"Excellent. I believe we go to Ackermann's about eleven."

"And your name?" he asked softly.

"Phillida Morgan, my lord. I am Lady Brookhaven's great-niece."

Lord John gazed blindly at the closed door, his body relaxed and his arm resting on the mantel but his thoughts hectic. Lady Brookhaven? The lady was a harpy of the old school who claimed the great Whig hostesses as friends. She was rumored to have several impressive lovers littering her past—although her affairs had not been quite so public as some and had not resulted in a plethora of half-related offspring.

Lady Brookhaven, in short, was not the chaperon he'd have chosen for a sprightly young miss with a mind of her own. Given her history, Lady Brookhaven was more likely to encourage her niece to throw her cap over the windmill than to keep a close guard over Miss Morgan's virtue! Then, too, Lord John was curious as to what the old harridan had said to turn the chit so firmly from himself!

Lord John plotted to discover the truth of it. He rather liked Phillida. He didn't think she was quite the sort he looked to make his wife—obviously not at all biddable—but that didn't mean he wished her to fall into the briars, which was all too likely if she were left to Lady Brookhaven's tender mercy! So. He'd have to bestir himself to assure such an inexperienced miss walked a narrow path. That would, unfortunately, be rather time-consuming just when he had determined to concentrate on finding himself a wife.

Wife. *Damnation,* he thought. He'd promised Tuttles he'd take a gander at Lady Gwendolyn and had yet to set eyes on the wench, let alone determine if she fell within the parameters he'd so blithely set! If only the first person he'd seen upon entering Lady Gavinthorpe's salon had not been that selfsame matchmaking mama who'd made his life miserable in the weeks before his valet left, he might not have immediately sequestered himself here in the library.

Lord John decided to put off meeting the first lady on Tuttles's list. Instead he'd find Lady Gavinthorpe, give her good eve, and be on his way. If he could do so without running into his nemesis, all would be well. Tomorrow he'd begin his surreptitious guardianship of the very green Phillida Morgan!

* * *

The next morning Miss Morgan followed her aunt, an indefatigable collector, around Ackermann's. She looked at prints when requested to do so, but otherwise indulged her own hobby. Phillida found far greater amusement in studying real people who were unaware they were being observed than in the modern obsession with prints and the collecting of them.

For instance, that lady in purple: the tightly laced body reminded Phillida of a pigeon, especially when she puffed her way up to a quarry and, by size alone, trapped the poor soul into conversation. Trailing behind was a wrenlike girl who appeared to exist in a dreamworld except when poked into a semblance of proper liveliness by the bigger bird, her mama. Across the room was another pair Phillida found intriguing. The woman was excessively tall and attempted to hide that fact in a most distressing fashion by lowering her head between hunched shoulders. Seated before her was an absentminded-looking soul, his graying locks tied back in an old-fashioned queue. He held an enlarging glass over one particular print, studying every inch. When the woman's sad eyes met hers, Phillida excused herself from her aunt's side.

"You look as lonely as I feel," said Phillida, holding out her hand to the tall female she'd watched with such interest. "I'm Phillida Morgan. Lady Brookhaven is my great-aunt, and I am a perfectly acceptable acquaintance for you to have"—she chuckled—"if you will, that is?"

The woman's mouth twitched and her eyes lightened. "I am Gwendolyn Troquair, only daughter of Lord Troquair, Earl of Troquair." Lady Gwendolyn bent her knees and rounded her back in an attempt to come down to Phillida's height. "As you may have guessed, my father is a scholar and, having exhausted every library within reach of our home, he chose to come to London for more Evidence for his Theory. We are staying for the nonce with his sister, who took me to Lady Gavinthorpe's soiree, which," she asked politely, "I believe you also attended?"

Phillida nodded. "I came to London at the invitation of my great-aunt. I *thought* she wished a companion, but I have discovered since I arrived she tricked me and wishes to marry me off. It is a distressing situation."

The sad eyes, a glimmer of disbelief in them now, met Phillida's. "You don't wish to marry?"

Phillida's laughter trilled. "I'm an odd creature, I believe." Briefly Phillida explained. "Are you looking for a husband?"

"I gave up all hopes of marriage many years ago," said Lady Gwendolyn in an airy tone which no one, least of all someone as perceptive as Phillida, would give the least credence.

"Then," said Phillida, wondering how she might help her new friend, "I propose we keep each other company at the many entertainments which I predict will be dreary in the extreme if I've no one with whom I may laugh. Ah, here is someone with whom I wish to speak," added Phillida. She waited until Lord John's gaze found hers, and smiled slightly.

Lord John sighed at such blatant invitation and shook his head at her. He moved around the room, speaking first to this person and then that, and, collecting Lady Cowper in passing, he approached his quarry. As he'd hoped, Lady Cowper knew one of the young ladies— but not the one he'd expected.

"Lady Gwendolyn Troquair, may I present Lord John?"

The required round of introductions continued, and Lord John was, at last, properly introduced to Phillida. In the meantime he found himself facing the first on

Tuttles's list and the bottom dropped out of his hopes. Certainly this cowering, stuttering woman would never do. His features, already set in stern lines on his arrival at Ackermann's, hardened, which, had he known it, only made Lady Gwendolyn's shyness worse.

How, he wondered, thoroughly exasperated, was he to separate Miss Morgan from Lady Gwendolyn and effect his invitation for the drive? For a moment—only a moment—he wished he'd not been so want-witted as to involve himself in Miss Morgan's affairs.

Three

In the end Lord Troquair solved Lord John's problem by rising from his chair and claiming his daughter's attention without a by-your-leave or the least awareness he interrupted a conversation. Miss Morgan called after them that they'd see one another that evening, and, as her father bore her off, Lady Gwendolyn nodded over her shoulder. Lord John exchanged a droll look with Lady Cowper at Lord Troquair's odd behavior before adroitly making his invitation to Miss Morgan for the drive. They strolled to where Lady Brookhaven stood with her favorite source of gossip.

Meeting her ladyship's narrowed gaze, Lord John smiled a bland smile and asked permission to take Miss Morgan for a turn around the Park. Lady Brookhaven, noting the interested bystanders, nodded once and turned away. She could not, thought Lord John smugly, have forbidden anything so innocuous as a drive—particularly not with someone so eligible as himself. Clearly she had *wished* to do so—which raised the question, again, of just what the lady planned for Miss Morgan's future. He was also, he reminded himself, curious as to what she had said to Miss Morgan to his detriment.

"Well, that went more smoothly than I'd thought it might." He lifted Phillida onto the high seat of his perch phaeton.

"Why should you have anticipated problems, my lord?" Phillida asked the question absently, much preoccupied by the odd sensations induced by his hands at her waist, sensations she'd never before felt—and then there was a shortness of breath which rather frightened her. . . . Was she coming down with some odd disease?

"You told me your aunt disapproved of me."

That caught Phillida's full attention. "I did? She does? I couldn't have done so. She's never suggested anything of the kind."

"She must have." Lord John's mouth formed a stubborn line. "She said something so malicious you immediately concluded I could not possibly be husband material and discarded me as a potential suitor for your hand."

"You must have misunderstood. All I said was that a marriage between us would not do." Lord John was obviously not satisfied with her response, but before he could question her, she added, "Now, will you please be serious? As it is, we have little time in which to lay plans—assuming you still wish to help me, of course." She turned a shrewd look his way.

The look confirmed the signs of intelligence he'd glimpsed the night before. The little Morgan, he decided, was nobody's fool—because he had, during the night watches, but only briefly, resented making the offer. "For reasons I've yet to explain to my own satisfaction, I find I do wish it. Perhaps I merely wish a diversion in what has promised to be a rather boring Season? In any case, we'd best get down to business. I assume you have in mind a particular sort of husband?" Lord John's brows rose higher and higher as Phillida gave a verbal sketch of the mythical man she believed might suit.

"And," she finished, "what I do not wish is the sort

Aunt Em believes proper for an ape leader such as myself."

"What sort is that, Miss Morgan?" asked Lord John. He was so intrigued by this decidedly self-assured young woman, he missed the inadvertently offered opportunity for a gentlemanly compliment denying her spinster status.

"My aunt seems to think that, because my father never traveled more than five miles from home once he'd settled at Briarton, I will be content with a bore with no interest beyond the state of his health or a clutch-fisted widower who will hide me away in the country to look after his monster brood by his first wife!"

Lord John chuckled. "No, that would not do. You require a man you may lead by the nose, of course. One who will not contradict you, ever, but will say yes, m'dear and no, m'dear, allowing you to go your own way."

"What a vicious thing to say to me, Lord John."

Her soft tone drew his gaze and he noted flashing eyes and the stubborn tilt to her chin. "Miss Morgan," he soothed, "if we are to deal together, you must learn when I am bamming you." But *had* he been jesting? he asked himself. No he had not. This was no demure and retiring miss who would allow her husband to rule the roost. Mendaciously he continued, "I no more think that sort will do you than will those Lady Brookhaven invites to inspect you."

Phillida, unaware he indulged in a social lie, relaxed. "I apologize, my lord, for jumping to conclusions. To whom *will* you introduce me?"

"Patience, Miss Morgan. You've only just listed your stipulations, and you must know they are other than one expects of a young lady on the hop for a husband. You insist fortune and looks are unimportant, but intelligence and a sense of humor are? Hmmm."

Lord John mulled over the possibles who came readily to mind. For some reason he was glad his team required his attention for the difficult turn into the Park. He avoided the popular drive down Rotten Row, choosing the path along the Serpentine. Why, he wondered, could he not bring to mind even one man who might suit? Not that he need find a candidate immediately— although he must do so before Lady Brookhaven achieved *her* goal.

Now why, he also wondered, was he so certain Miss Morgan's aunt was playing an underhanded game with her young relative? His first notion, that, although herself a trifle loose in the haft, her ladyship would be so reprehensible as to guide her relative down the garden path, was surely an unwarranted assumption. Which left what? It appeared he must spend a great deal of time with Miss Morgan if he were to discover the truth of it—and if he were to help Miss Morgan achieve her goals, of course.

"Where are you to be found this evening, Miss Morgan? For that matter, where will you be any time the next few days?"

Obligingly, Phillida told him, but, again, she wondered at his reason for befriending her. That he might be *used*, as she'd blithely suggested in Lady Gavinthorpe's library, was unlikely, so why *was* he cooperating? Any notion he might find her personally interesting was laughable. Although she wasn't, she hoped, an antidote, she'd no particular claim to beauty, and although she had an easy competence to rely on, Lord John had a more than adequate fortune of his own. It wasn't marriage. He was known, or so her aunt insisted, to avoid marriage, perfectly content with some barque of

frailty—blonds, each and every one—which she was
not. It was certainly a mystery.

After one or two glances at her frowning face, Lord
John suggested, "You've become excessively serious."

"It just occurred to me it was excessively fast of me
to ask for your help. That bothers me less than it ought,
perhaps, but, having admitted I should *not* have asked,
I can't help wondering why you have agreed."

"Very blunt, Miss Morgan." A muscle tripped over in
his jaw, jerked a second time.

"You are angry with me. I'd apologize and say it was
none of my business, but, my lord, you must admit it *is*."

He chuckled at her earnestness. "I am not angry with
you, Miss Morgan, but annoyed with myself. I am not,
I freely admit, open to every odd suggestion made to
me. Nor am I known as one who gallants the young and
innocent." An arrested look crossed his features. He
turned to stare at her. "Do you suppose that, by doing so
now, we'll give rise to just the sort of gossip amongst
the old cats which I abhor?"

"Of course we will!" she said, much struck. "We
would not wish anyone to jump to a wrongheaded conclusion. That would, indeed, be too bad." He feared she
was about to suggest they call their arrangement off and
found it an unacceptable solution, so he was both surprised and pleased when she added: "Let me try if I can
find a believable excuse which you may put around."

Phillida screwed up her forehead in a most delectable
fashion. Lord John, noting the delightful expression, remembered he was a gentleman and manfully restrained
himself from immediately turning her into his arms so
he might soothe away such obvious agitation. What a
comfortable armful she'd be, too, he thought, his eyes
straying with rather less restraint. Her voice broke into
suddenly emerging notions he knew were best interrupted.

"In the Peninsula, did you, perhaps, meet Obrey Masterson? He was a second lieutenant in the Fifty-second Rifles."

"Masterson . . . ," Lord John repeated the name. "Now what do I know of . . . aha! He died not quite a year ago now, I think?" She nodded. "At Ciudad Rodrigo. A hotheaded hero, he volunteered for a forlorn hope that was, I fear, forlorn indeed—although essential to the success of the planned assault. He was a particular friend of yours?"

"Well"—the dimple came and went—"now he is safely dead, I suppose I may claim to have been nearly acquainted with him—assuming you are willing to remember a promise to him, concerning me, which you had forgotten until now and you find yourself obliged to ease my way into the ton because of it?"

"I do not care to figure as a man who forgets his promises," he objected, "but isn't it entirely possible he did me some service during our mutual stay in the Peninsula which I now repay by easing your way?"

"Very good, m'lord."

"I'm glad you approve, Miss Morgan," he said, his visage properly impassive.

Phillida glanced at him, and he, sliding his eyes sideways, met her look. They broke into mutual chuckles, surprising one or two equestrians into taking a second look at the young and, one had thought, not particularly interesting lady in Lord John's phaeton.

"I was surprised to see Lord John at this soiree," said Lady Brookhaven much later that night as she accepted her footman's help and climbed into her carriage for the short drive back to Herrick Square. She waited until her niece settled herself before adding, "It is known he avoids Society's tamer entertainments." When this brought no response, her ladyship poked Phillida with her fan. "I'm talking to you, missy."

"Hmmm? Oh. Lord John. Yes, I, too, was surprised. He believes he's discovered a way of paying off a debt he feels he owes a mutual friend."

"Piffle."

"Oh, dear." Phillida chuckled. "What can I have said to elicit such an ill-bred response?"

Lady Brookhaven ignored her irrepressible niece's impertinence. She was single-minded in her determination to terminate a situation she feared would play havoc with her plans. "Lord John does not pay attention to marriageable young ladies. Never. And if he were to begin, he'd not find it necessary to dream up convenient debts in order to scratch up an acquaintance. You mark my words, m'girl, a man of that stamp has only one thing in mind when he pays a woman distinguishing attentions."

Lady Brookhaven now deplored that Phillida had that physical aura which she'd originally thought an advantage. If Lord John were to change his rule about blonds and take up with her dark-haired niece, she must push ahead quickly. Any friendship with Lord John must be nipped in the bud.

"One wrong step, m'dear," said her ladyship, syrup dripping from her tongue, "and you'll find yourself flat on your back. You'll be ruined." Lady Brookhaven swore at the flickering light from quickly passed flambeaus and street lamps which made it difficult to see her niece's expression. Had she managed to frighten the chit?

Phillida stifled a wish to strangle her relation who, once again, was putting her to the blush with words too blunt for innocent ears. "You err," she said crisply. "I am not the sort to catch an out-and-outer's eye."

Lady Brookhaven wondered if the girl could possibly

be that unaware of her attractions. Surely it was impossible. . . .

"It is quite simple, really. I don't know if my mother ever mentioned the Mastersons in her letters to you?" Lady Brookhaven was startled by the seeming non sequitur, but, after a moment's thought, nodded. "Then you will remember Obrey Masterson's father and mine had a mutual passion for the classics?" That much was true. Now for the deceit on which the arrangement between Lord John and herself was based. "Obrey saved Lord John's, er, bacon, at the battle of Ciudad Rodrigo. He insists that since Obrey and I were great friends"— another lie—"he has discovered a way of paying that debt. He will, he says, ease me into the highest circles."

Lady Brookhaven snorted. "Something of which *I* am incapable, of course."

"Oh, dear. Has his decision to help bear-lead me through social jungles put your nose out of joint, my lady?" asked the lady's undutiful niece.

"That's enough impertinence, missy." Lady Brookhaven's eyes glittered icily until Phillida, hiding her amusement, lowered her gaze demurely. "Believe me," the old lady continued, "when such as Lord John sets his eyes to a woman, she'd best be on guard. I assure you the game is too deep for you, the stakes too high."

"I am more than seven, my lady, and I know when a man is setting up a flirtation. There's no sign of it," insisted Phillida.

Was that wistfulness in her niece's voice? Lady Brookhaven wished she were less tired. Here was much in need of sifting. If her buffle-headed niece were to set her sights as high as Lord John, then all efforts to guide the gel toward the husband chosen for her would be set at naught.

Introducing Phillida to the most boring of men was the first step in Lady Brookhaven's plan. By doing so, she expected Phillida to feel relief when she met Lady Brookhaven's grandson. The dratted boy was a bore, as well, but a well-looking and young bore. It was important she get the silly chub a strong wife, one who would shake out the odd notions to which he stubbornly held and, most important of all, bring him into the Party where young blood was needed. Having decided Phillida was the woman, Lady Brookhaven would tolerate no interference. Her grandson must get his head out of the muck as ordered and get himself into Town for the Season! Pig farming indeed!

"What are our plans for tomorrow?" asked the old lady querulously.

"Hmm?" Phillida stifled a yawn. "I believe we are promised to Lady Gavinthorpe again. Dinner and the opera?"

"Drat." Lady Brookhaven bit the tip of her little finger. She couldn't cancel a dinner engagement. Not at this late date. But then, Lord John was unlikely to have an invitation. They would go to dinner. She'd decide later about the opera, where chances were greater they'd meet the man whom she wished, above all others, to avoid.

"Well?" asked Mr. Porterman, his curiosity obvious.

Tuttles heaved a lugubrious and decidedly overdone sigh. "Not well at all, m'friend—although Lord John has met our quarry. *That* information was by the way when his lordship honored me with the story of his introduction to our red herring. It seems he took poor Lady Gwendolyn in deep disgust and wonders if I've slipped a few bones in the old box." Tuttles put on an air of sadness. "What is the world coming to that such young twerps are so lacking in respect to one of my years?" Controlling chortles, Porterman accepted a newly filled tankard from his friend. "Ah, Missus Flint. Well met."

"I cannot stay above the moment. I only wish to report that our plans are moving along. My miss has yet to meet the decoy, but she's met Lord John. I don't know how they've managed to fall in with each other so smoothly, but it's not quite as we planned." Flint frowned. "She's asked him to introduce her to men she might find tolerable in the marriage bond!"

The three conspirators cast worried glances from one to another. "You conclude she thinks Lord John would *not* do?" asked Porterman cautiously.

"She has taken the notion Lord John is a debauched soul, and that she cannot see herself in the role of complacent wife." Tuttles bristled at the insult to his master. "And she added a new requirement to her list."

"Which is?"

"She says the gentleman she chooses must not be deep in petticoat country." She looked from her father to his friend. "When she added her new restriction, she said it with such a sad look as you wouldn't believe."

"Actually," said Tuttles, coming down out of the boughs, "if she's sad, that may be a good sign, might it not?" Everyone looked thoughtful. After a moment's silence, Tuttles added, "Lord John also has a new requirement. He has decided his wife must not have an excess of relatives."

Flint hid a smile. She could certainly sympathize. No one would, by choice, add Lady Brookhaven to one's family tree—even as a mere connection.

"If you're wishful to stir up the pot, I've a pair of names you might give our flats," said her father before disappearing into his tankard. When encouraged, he said, "Suggest Sir Romney to Miss Morgan. He's thirty-two, a widower with one child—a son on whom he dotes. He is not on the catch for a wife, but he likes to talk about the boy."

"Sir Romney? I once knew him." Flint's eyes narrowed. "Lady John maneuvered him into a marriage he did not want, and, by doing so, broke the heart of the poor miss I dressed then. If one were to talk of relatives to be avoided, there is one!"

Mr. Porterman patted her hand in sympathy and went on portentously. "If Lord John attends the opera this evening, he should look for Lady Pretherwhit. She bearleads a granddaughter who is an avowed bluestocking with advanced notions in her cockloft, such as extending the suffrage and prison reform. She's young for our purposes, but dresses badly and her dowdy appearance makes her seem older—or so says her despairing maid. She's not exactly as ugly as a thunder-mug, but she don't appear her best, neither, since she won't bother." Porterman paused. "She's an excellent musician, however, playing the pianoforte and the viola and a true lover of music, which may appeal to his lordship until he discovers her other foibles."

"However did you find out so much?" asked Flint, an admiring note in her voice. "She sounds a perfect diversion until we can manage to make my miss and Mr. Tuttles's master take a proper look at each other."

"You've done well, old friend," agreed Tuttles. "I will trot along and find an occasion to pass the word to Lord John. May I escort you, missus?"

"I'd like that, Mr. Tuttles, but we'd best hurry, since I'm on a mission of mercy and have been gone too long already." The men politely pretended they were not interested, and Flint chuckled. "I've bought the ingredients for a tisane to be made to Miss Morgan's orders for the second housemaid's headache. She is kindhearted to notice, is she not? My miss," she finished, "is a proper lady and deserving of the very best we can do for her."

"I do wish your daughter could be brought to a proper understanding of priorities, Porterman," said Tuttles just a trifle peevishly. "It is *his lordship* who is deserving of the best."

Porterman laughed. "It's better than a play watching the two of you bristle and brood. You'll be the death of me, the way each of you goes on the hop when the other so much as blinks crosswise." He chortled, chortled still more at his friend's nose-in-the-air leave-taking.

Phillida, seated in the Gavinthorpe box at the Royal Opera, did her best not to gawk as if she were an impressionable girl. The brilliant lighting from hundreds of candles was shattered into a myriad of colors by the crystal drops of the chandeliers which hung on arms out from the tiers; gilding gleamed against white paint; sumptuous scarlet drapery enriched the boxes . . . everything dazzled the eye. Then, when one searched for friends and acquaintances, one was further bemused by the clothes and jewels. Phillida wished her escort would stop his monologue long enough that she might take it in.

". . . So you see, Miss Morgan, the theaters are always in danger of fire. Not that it is likely another disgruntled musician will deliberately set fire to the Opera House, as is believed to have happened the last time it burned. You would like to know that Robert Smirke took in hand this reconstruction in the new Greek Doric style," he finished in his usual instructive style.

"If we are in such danger, then why do we come?" asked Phillida. She discovered Lady Gwendolyn sitting farther back and one level up. She wriggled her fingers and received a smile in return.

Ignoring her question, he continued, "Now, look you at the proscenium. That's the bit—"

Phillida's patience gave out and, although it was beyond the line of being pleasing, she couldn't resist giving the man a set-down. "I know what a proscenium is, Mr. Dipplewood. Please cease treating me like a child who must be instructed in the most basic facts. Perhaps you aren't aware my father was a scholar. I assure you, he saw to it that I was well taught."

"Well taught!" He goggled at her. "But you're a *female*."

"So I've believed all my life."

He ignored her dry humor. "I've been misled as to your character, Miss Morgan." Mr. Dipplewood lowered his voice, but his tone remained portentous: "I cannot like subterfuge. I tell you now so that you will not build airdreams: I will never offer for an educated woman."

"What a relief, Mr. Dipplewood. I feel certain we would not suit."

"You put a good face on it. That is excellent. I sincerely hope your heart is not too badly bruised."

Phillida turned to look at her escort. *He was serious.* "I will recover from any bruising you've done—except perhaps to my ears. Please lower your voice if you cannot be still: the performance is about to begin."

Phillida, who had never seen an opera, was entranced by the drama and music as well as the sets, which, she'd heard, were particularly good. Well taught as she was, she could follow the Italian in which the performance was presented. Therefore, at the first interval she woke as from a dream, her eyes sparkling. Leaning forward during a lull in the conversation between her aunt and Lady Gavinthorpe, she touched her hostess lightly on the shoulder. "Thank you so much for the opportunity to hear such music," she said. "Opera hasn't come my way before. I'm enjoying the performance very much indeed."

Lady Brookhaven turned in her chair and stared at her niece. "Enjoying-the-performance," she said, and repeated herself on a higher note: "*Enjoying-the-performance*. Don't you know, you ninny, you don't come to the opera to enjoy the performance?"

"Some do," responded Phillida, her eyes moving toward one of the larger boxes, a Lord Fairweather's, in the tier rising directly from the stage.

Lord Fairweather was a patron of the opera. Phillida had been surprised to discover Lord John amongst his guests when she'd scanned the theater. She'd felt a burning sensation deep inside upon noticing he was deep in conversation with a badly dressed young woman. Then she'd laughed softly in her attitude, which, she assured herself, was dog-in-manger. She didn't wish him for herself, so why was she upset? She looked around as Lady Gwendolyn entered the box on the arm of a gentleman Phillida had not yet met.

"My dear friend," Gwendolyn said to her, "may I introduce Mr. Diggory?"

Phillida blinked. This was Mr. Diggory? The Quakerish gentleman her maid had suggested as a possible husband? Phillida joined in the ensuing conversation, ignoring, as much as possible, Mr. Dipplewood, who continued making an exhibition of himself by talking of things he did not understand.

So this was Mr. Diggory. He was not a tall man—in fact, he was shorter than Lady Gwendolyn, although that did not seem to bother either the gentleman or her friend, a surprise, as Gwen was usually so terribly unhappy about her height. Mr. Diggory's hair was receding but not in an unattractive way, his countenance was pleasing, but, most important, he talked like a sensible man—something Phillida appreciated after being subjected to Mr. Dipplewood all evening. Setting one thing against another, Phillida was prone to approve. But not for herself.

Lady Gavinthorpe requested lemonade. Phillida breathed more freely once Mr. Dipplewood left her side, but very shortly her breath caught sharply as Lord John and the dowdy lady pushed aside the curtain and entered the box. He made the introductions between Lady Elizabeth and the others and, setting Mr. Diggory, Lady Elizabeth, and Lady Gwendolyn to arguing over the performance of a secondary character in the opera, he maneuvered Phillida into the corner.

"Who is the court-card escorting you this evening?" he asked, amusement obvious.

Phillida searched for the faintest hint of the jealousy she'd felt when seeing him engrossed by Lady Elizabeth. She found none. "Mr. Dipplewood is one of those creatures my aunt feels suitable. She must be disappointed, I fear. He's informed me that, although he does not wish to bruise my heart, allowing me to hope would be unfair. Mr. Dipplewood would *never* do a thing so unseemly as offer for an educated woman. He will not again be gracing Aunt Emily's salon . . . I hope!"

Lord John's shout of laughter turned heads. He ignored the fact that he'd brought unwanted attention onto the Gavinthorpe box—if he noticed it—and lifted Phillida's hand for a kiss observed by half the ton. "You are a minx, m'dear," he said softly, still holding her hand for all to see. "A minx and a delight. Don't change," he added quite seriously.

Phillida's gaze was trapped. She had grave difficulty swallowing. Again she suffered those odd sensations. She was grateful—well, nearly so—for Mr. Dipplewood's return with a footman bearing a tray of glasses. Noting Lord John's interest in Phillida, Mr. Dipplewood boggled, the glass in his hand tipped, and cold liquid spilled onto Phillida's gown.

"Oh, deary me," said the culprit, embarrassed that one of the leaders of the ton should have observed such clumsiness. He dabbed at the stain with a none-too-clean handkerchief. Lord John elbowed him away, his lips a stern line. "How can I have been so awkward? Ohdearohdearohdear." Mr. Dipplewood looked around anxiously, but no one was attending to him.

"I believe you should go home, Miss Morgan. You can't be comfortable," said Lord John. "If your aunt will trust you to my care, I'll escort you."

"That will not be necessary, my lord," said Lady Brookhaven, indicating she'd kept track of what was going forward. "I am not enjoying this performance"— it was unclear whether she meant the one on the stage or what was transpiring in the box—"at all." She made their apologies to Lady Gavinthorpe and swept her niece away before more words could be exchanged with the infuriating Lord John.

The salon was empty of guests when Lady Gwendolyn arrived in the gray drizzle of a new day. Phillida discovered her friend was not so shy as to be unable to reply to Lady Brookhaven's catechism into her background and prospects. Lady Brookhaven, having discovered more than was necessary if not all she wished, turned to greet friends who would inform her of the newest on *dits*, thus allowing Phillida to escape to a corner with *her* friend.

"I must apologize for my overbearing relative," said Phillida, covering her embarrassment with a light tone.

"I know just how it is," agreed Lady Gwendolyn. "My father doesn't pry into what is not his business. It is *worse* that he totally ignores even the most basic conventions of common politeness. I suppose everyone has at least one relative to put them to the blush."

Before their visit ended, the young women were on much easier terms. As they shook hands upon leave-taking, Phillida suggested they go shopping the next day. Lady Brookhaven added her invitation and nearly ruined all before it became clear she, herself, would not be going. Lady Gwendolyn immediately remembered she would *not*, as she had thought, be too busy for such a treat.

The salon was temporarily deserted. Lady Brook-haven took the opportunity to congratulate Phillida on her new friend. "You haven't such looks you may asso-ciate with just any woman. Lady Gwendolyn, pie-faced as she is, sets off your mediocre physiognomy very well indeed."

Phillida's temper rose at the suggestion she was tak-ing up Gwendolyn merely as a foil to herself. Before she could get control of the growing rage and put her tongue around words of suitably scathing nature, visi-tors were announced—including the biggest bore amongst the bores to whom she'd been introduced. She gave the short, well-corseted gentleman two fingers.

"You will be wondering why I have not come before to give you proper attentions, Miss Morgan," said Mr. Womsley once the proprieties had been seen to. "I wish to explain," he began . . .

. . . only to lose Phillida's attention when Lord John was announced. He strolled into Lady Brookhaven's salon as if he'd done it often over the years. Lord John made only the briefest of bows to her ladyship before crossing the room to Phillida's side.

"Sorry I'm late," he said, looking through his glass at Mr. Womsley before turning back to Phillida in such a way that he excluded the other from their conversation. "Be a good girl and fetch your pelisse. There's a sharpish breeze now the rain's stopped, and I don't wish to keep my horses standing."

Mr. Womsley opened and closed his mouth in such a way that his resemblance to a landed fish—a very plump fish—upset Phillida's equilibrium. Half strangled with laughter, she said good-bye to him, pretended she didn't hear her aunt's sharp words, and left the room. She barely managed to shut the door before collapsing against the wall, where she held her sides and chortled. *Oh!, dear,* she thought, *I must discover a way of controlling my abominable sense of the ridiculous, or one day I'll disgrace myself!*

She hurried up to her room where Flint insisted she change into a newly arrived carriage dress of the finest Irish linen with many tucks and matching ecru ribbons running through embroidered eyelets.

"Must I?"

"It would be considered proper."

"Lord John doesn't wish to keep his horses standing," objected Phillida a bit later when Flint pushed her down before her mirror and to restyle her hair.

"You do not wish to appear forward, do you?" hinted Flint.

Phillida was much struck by the common sense of that and complied with more docility. Something over twenty minutes later, she returned to where Lord John waited in the hall. As she neared the bottom step, he pulled out his watch.

"Very good. I predicted a full half hour. I don't know how you achieved such a magnificent effect so quickly, but I compliment you." He flicked the brim of her bonnet with a careless finger before offering his arm

So much for making his lordship wait, thought Phillida.

Four

Something, Phillida thought, *must be wrong. These odd feelings whenever he touches me cannot be normal. Especially when he lifts me.* She removed her hands from his shoulders the instant she was settled into his phaeton. *This is—well, it's annoying,* she decided, not quite certain that was the word for which she searched.

They threaded their way through the streets toward Hyde Park. Phillida loved watching Lord John's easy handling of the flighty team. When certain she'd not interfere with his concentration, she said, "I must thank you for the adroitness of your rescue, Lord John."

"That particular situation was no test of my mettle, Miss Morgan. Did I, however, detect a certain simmering anger in your aunt as I said good-bye? Is she seriously expecting you to honey up to that pompous little idiot?"

"Honey up to? My lord, I'm sure I haven't a notion what you mean by that phrase, and," she raised a hand when he seemed about to explain, "I'm very sure I've no desire to know. If, however, you're asking if Aunt Em thinks him a proper suitor, then"—Phillida frowned—"I cannot answer. She doesn't discourage him, but she hasn't touted him to me either. I think she would if she wished me to consider him seriously."

"Which gives one to wonder what she is up to. Something, to be sure."

"Why do you think that? I've made it clear I've no wish for a husband. She's made it equally clear I should look about me for one. She introduces me to every bore in town, but leaves it up to me to pursue the acquaintance." Phillida frowned thoughtfully. "That tactful lack of interference sounds very unlike my overbearing aunt, does it not?" she asked after a moment.

Lord John gave her the sort of look one gives a child who has performed beyond his expected capability. "I do like the fact you have a mind which functions logically, Miss Morgan. Your explanation smells of fish," he added, "because it's not in character. Your aunt, Miss Morgan, plays with loaded dice."

"What an interesting conclusion, my lord." Phillida was miffed by his obvious expectation that a feminine mind was generally filled with air. "My aunt says the same of *you*, although not," she added, "in quite those words."

Lord John's features twisted in an expression of angry denial. "How dare that woman hand out insults?"

"I daresay because she has the same traits of character which allow you to insult her, my lord."

He reined in and turned a cold eye on her. "And that is?" he asked.

Phillida adopted a pose of wide-eyed innocence—spoiled, if she'd known, by the flickering appearance of a dimple. "It's one all tonish people have in common, my lord." Did she dare go on? *Ah, well. In for a penny* . . . she thought. "I've noticed again and again the belief you are born to rule, born knowing the right of things, and surprised if anyone disagrees."

Lord John blinked. He blinked again. "But . . ."

"Yes, my lord?" she asked, her voice as demure as her angelic features.

His eyes widened. Finally he said, "You *serpent*."

"Me, my lord?"

"You did that deliberately."

"Did what deliberately?"

"You set me up and knocked me down and left me on the mat looking at sky. How *dare* you?"

"Isn't that obvious? I, too, am a member of the ton, Lord John. I, too, believe myself always in the right."

"But not born to rule?" he asked slyly. His smile widened when she shook her head. "Admit it. The man you wish found for you will *not* be a retiring country gentleman who never sees beyond the end of his nose. Perhaps a political gentleman?"

"It's certainly true I require a man who has something other than the set of his coat or the planting of his acres to occupy his mind. How did you guess?"

"Because the sort you mention would bore you to death in no time."

"And have you decided upon someone who will not bore me?"

"I had a man in mind," he said, tongue in cheek, "but he is, alas, too preoccupied with the folds of his cravat to be interested in marriage. He is determined to invent a fashion which may carry his name, you see." Phillida turned disbelieving eyes on her escort. "It is quite true. He failed in an earlier effort to introduce cabbage-sized pompoms on dancing slippers."

"You are, once again, cutting a wheedle, my lord. I begin to wonder if you were serious about aiding my search. For instance, I'm sure you know that particular gentleman." She raised one finger from her clasped hands and pointed, returning her hands to their former demure position before anyone could note the impoliteness.

"Brummel is not on the catch for a wife," said Lord John.

"I'm not so green I don't know that. But I've heard he has even greater sway than you when it comes to setting one's feet on the path to success in the ton. You might introduce me, my lord."

"Your aunt wouldn't approve," said Lord John, repressively.

"How one may be mistaken in another. I hadn't guessed you *wished* to gain my aunt's approval, my lord." He didn't respond, but his lips compressed. "You will not introduce us?" He lifted his reins slightly and his team quickened their pace. "Ah, well. Too late. We have passed him. You do not approve of the Beau, my lord? How sorry I feel for him. Poor man."

"There is nothing poor about him except his pocket-book, Miss Morgan. He rose from nothing—his father was *not*, however, a valet, as is sometimes rumored—to make a place for himself. He begins to think himself omniscient and believes his position unassailable. He'll discover his mistake someday when he goes too far and finds himself in Prinny's black book. The Prince made him by taking him up. The Prince will eventually break him."

"Does your prediction mean you feel omniscient, my lord?" He turned a wary look her way, and she chuckled. He grinned, lifting the hand which held the whip in salute, but said nothing.

Phillida continued in a serious vein. "You are giving me more evidence for what I've come to believe during my admittedly short stay in the so-called best of circles. The ton is fickle and without conscience and takes such things as friendship and loyalty lightly, does it not? That man has done much to improve Society. But the least slip and Society will banish him. I find it a world I cannot like."

"Much of Society is fickle, Miss Morgan, because it is bored and needs constant distraction. I won't argue that point. But, believe me, there is another, better, side to it, which I hope to show you before the Season ends.

What, by the way, has Brummel done to improve Society?"

"But isn't it obvious, my lord?" He shook his head. Phillida sighed and explained: "He designed attire which makes men look like men instead of gaudy birds—as was the style not many years ago—but more important, he introduced the notion of cleanliness! The last alone should make him an earl on the next honors list, should it not?"

Lord John's obvious enjoyment of the young lady ensconced in his carriage, his laughter, and crinkled-up eyes, were noted by a number of tonish gentlemen. Several became deeply involved in an argument concerning the lady. It was suggested that Lord John had, at long last, been caught in Cupid's velvet trap. The opposite was argued by others who had heard a rumor she was the friend of an officer who had placed Lord John under an obligation and that he was merely paying the debt by doing the pretty by the friend's ladylove. Bets were laid, the odds argued, all wagers to be decided by the status of the two at the end of the Season.

"Do pull up," said Miss Morgan, her hand laid briefly on her escort's well-muscled arm. For a moment she was distracted, when once again she experienced that sensation which bothered her so much. "I see someone you know," she added when his questioning look recalled her wandering wits. "Tell me who is walking with Lady Pretherwhit and Lady Elizabeth? And why do they look so glum, do you suppose?"

"You'd look glum, too, listening to Sir Romney, Miss Morgan. The man's only conversation is of his son." Nevertheless, Lord John pulled up his team.

Later that afternoon, Lord John discovered Lady Elizabeth was on his butler's list of possible brides. "No."

"No, m'lord?"

"Definitely not. Are you aware the young woman is so blue I daresay she can't open her mouth without giving herself away?"

"How did you discover *that* if she don't speak?" asked Tuttles, rattled.

"Because she *does* dare. Foolish chit!"

Tuttles sighed. Another red herring wasted. They definitely must do better if they were to bring Miss Morgan and his lordship to take a serious look at each other. "M'lord, may I ask where you came across the young lady?"

"At the opera last night. I visited Fairweather's box, as is my custom. Lady Elizabeth and her grandmother were among his guests. Then I met her again today in the Park when driving out with Miss Morgan, a young relative of Lady Brookhaven."

Tuttles bowed more deeply than the response to his impertinent question required, but he needed, desperately, to hide his expression: if Lord John was taking Miss Morgan for drives, their plan was not, perhaps, so far off the mark as they'd thought. "I will endeavor to do better, m'lord. Surely I can find some woman who would make you a bride of whom you can be proud."

Lord John's brows rose. "Why, Tuttles, did I say she must be someone of whom I may be proud?"

"We'll be unable to meet the next day or two," said Tuttles morosely. "Lady John comes to town—unless she changes her mind. She does that."

"She's a difficult mistress?" asked Flint, sympathy in her tone.

"Difficult? A tartar, forever contradicting herself and ever demanding the impossible. One could deal with that if it were the worst."

"It isn't?" Flint's expression invited confidences.

"No. *Far* worse is that she upsets Lord John. It's sad how the wrong woman can turn the nicest of masters into a tyrant and an imbecile."

Flint laughed. "Is it possible to be both at the same time?"

"It is *because* she makes him a gibbering idiot he acts the tyrant."

"Explain that."

"Her nagging is the worst," said Tuttles, rubbing his chin. "Take her insistence he marry and beget an heir, f'instance."

"Something we've *not* been taking seriously, o' course," suggested Mr. Porterman, disappearing into his nearly empty mug to avoid retribution.

"It isn't the same," said Tuttles, and Flint nodded agreement. "In the first place," he continued, "we've been *asked* to do something—which Lady John has not— and in the second we don't shrew at him. And what's more," he added as a clincher, "we've got his best interests at heart."

"There's no arguing with you, I see," said Porterman, chuckling softly.

Flint met her father's eyes. "I see what you're saying, Father, and agree that manipulating them may not be the thing, but I also agree with Mr. Tuttles that we only want the best for them. From what I know of Lady John, it's very likely his lordship's interests are of no importance at all."

"I don't know how you know that, but it's true enough," said Tuttles.

"I told you that I once worked for a lady who had her heart set on Sir Romney. He'd given every indication he was near to popping the question, when Lady John took a hand." Her father reached over and patted her knee when her rising temper at the old hurt became obvious.

"There was a cousin, you see, an older girl of no particular distinction. Lady John decided to marry her off. She chose Sir Romney. The man was leg-shackled to the wrong lady before the cat could clean its whiskers."

"But what did Lady John do?"

"At first she played on the gentleman's kind heart, asking him to escort her little cousin here and there, which he did for pity's sake. Then she talked and talked and told him, at the last, how her poor cousin's heart would break if he did not offer for her after raising her hopes."

"And what happened to *your* young lady?"

"She went into a bit of a decline and, later, refused to marry. Her father died destitute and left her nothing, so, having come down in the world, she went to a great-aunt in Tunbridge Wells and very likely runs errands and takes fat pugs for walks and can't call her soul her own. Poor dear."

"Perhaps," suggested Tuttles, teasing, "when we've achieved our goal with Lord John and Miss Morgan, we may turn our minds to that little problem."

Flint blushed. "Now give over, do. I can't be gone much longer. That's old history and we've things to decide."

"We need a new plan," said Tuttles, "and I'll have little time for plotting. We must be prepared, for fear Lady John keeps to her present plan." The hangdog air he'd lost in their bantering, returned. "I hope my luck is in and her ladyship remains in the country!"

Later that evening, Lord John lowered his champagne glass and stared rudely across the heads of the couple with whom he'd been talking. The man didn't notice, continuing his diatribe against Tory interference in

Pinny's feud with his wife. The speaker's wife, more observant, tugged at her husband's sleeve.

"Madam," said that portly gentleman, "you interrupt me."

"I believe," she whispered, "Lord John is preoccupied with something other than our dear Prince's problems."

"Nonsense. Nothing is of more interest than Pinny's difficulties."

Mr. Morrison took a better look at his quarry, whom he had trapped into a corner. Then, unable to turn his head due to the height of cravat and collar points, he turned his whole body to see what it was which made Lord John frown so. He was not a tall man and could not see over the heads of people between himself and the entrance. He turned back to Lord John and sighed. Whatever was holding his lordship's attention, Mr. Morrison had, indeed, lost it.

Lord John said, "I apologize for seeing no solution to the problem, Mr. Morrison. I will put my mind to your question when I've a moment or two to spare. Just now I must tend to something more urgent. Excuse me."

Lord John bowed to Mrs. Morrison, bowed less deeply to the bore who was gobbling at the notion anything could be more urgent than his Prince's problems. He slid to one side, escaping the trap in which he'd allowed himself to be caught—quite aware that no matchmaking mama with a sweet innocent at her heels would intrude on one of Mr. Morrison's long-winded and overly frank discussions of Pinny's conjugal problems.

Lord John hovered near the circle Lady Brookhaven dominated. Trailing her ladyship were Miss Morgan and a countrified young gentleman who looked around in a bemused fashion. It took Lord John several moments to put a name to a man who was rarely found in town, but, finally, he'd recognized her ladyship's grandson, Osboure Linwood, Lord Brookhaven. The mystery of the lady's plot was solved. Lord John wondered if Miss Morgan had tumbled to the design of it yet. If not, he'd feel not the slightest guilt at informing her ladyship's great-niece of her ladyship's plan.

Lord John waited until one of Lady Brookhaven's cronies—obviously full of news—trotted up. Then, deftly, he separated Miss Morgan from her relatives, leading her into the supper room where they might be expected to find her a glass of fruit punch or a lemonade.

"I told you your aunt had a card or two up her sleeve."

Phillida was amusing herself by watching the flirtation between a carefully maquillaged woman of uncertain age and a roué of similar years who was powdered and patched in the style of an earlier generation and who tottered around the silver-headed cane on which he rested both gnarled hands. She blinked. "My lord? You spoke?"

"You are so good for my self-esteem, Miss Morgan."

"I am?" Phillida glanced up at the man who was beginning to intrude into far too many hours of introspection. "Ah. I see. A salutary lesson which is long overdue, think you?" She batted her long lashes in mimicry of a young girl flirting with her beau.

He ignored the gambit. "I've yet to determine if it is *salutary,* but I freely admit I've never been ignored so often or so obviously by anyone else."

"Definitely salutary. One can become too used to having one's every word attended to as if each were a gem of rare price. It would, eventually, go to one's head with the saddest results."

"Do I, I wonder, dare?" He seemed to contemplate the question. "I do. Trembling, but, with great bravery, I ask: what results, Miss Morgan?"

"But think!" She opened her eyes wide. "One would be required at unexpected intervals to buy new hats. *Most* embarrassing if one's head swelled when one wasn't paying attention and one discovered one had not a single hat which fit just when one was most needed."

"I feared it."

"I thought I might just give you a hint, but I see it isn't needed. I knew you were bright as a new guinea, my lord." It was Phillida's turn to treat the gentleman like a particularly intelligent child.

"I feared I shouldn't ask," he elaborated.

Phillida shook her head, a mournful air about her. "I was mistaken. Not bright at all."

"No. Particularly dense, in fact, for not guessing the reason for Lady Brookhaven's invitation which, my dear delight, brought you to London for a Season. If, that is, I may change this interesting conversation to one less damaging to my badly bruised image?" Curious, she nodded. "Then, to repeat what you missed earlier, I have uncovered a deep-dyed plot."

Phillida blinked. "You have?" She tipped her head to one side like a cheeky sparrow, a delightful indication she was attempting to discover his meaning.

Lord John waited, amused by the various expressions flitting over Miss Morgan's expressive features. But time was passing, so he interrupted her cogitations. "You've been set up, my dear," he said kindly.

"Set up? What can you mean?" Her eyes flashed to meet his, and she asked, "Is that cant, my lord?"

It was Lord John's turn to frown slightly. "Do you know, I cannot tell you. What it means, however, is that you have been placed just so in order to fulfill some design." When she still didn't tumble to the truth, he sighed. "In this case, my sweet innocent, marriage to Lady Brookhaven's callow grandson. Lady Brookhaven has decided you will make your cloddish cousin a suitable wife."

"Marriage? To Osbourn?" Phillida laughed. When Lord John remained sober, nodding his head ever so slightly, she stared. "But you cannot be serious." She blinked when he still didn't smile or give any indication he was hoaxing her. "Good heavens. You *do* mean it." He nodded portentously. "She nags him to take his place in the House of Lords. You can't imagine the arguments!"

"Taking his seat may be a part of her plan, Miss Morgan, but it is as plain as the delightful nose on your face she hopes to turn you into a proper bear-leader for her young cub. She expects you to marry him."

"How ridiculous. I have at least two years in my dish more than he. And, forgetting those years, I am a hundred years his senior in other ways. Besides which he is a bore who, when allowed to choose the topic, can talk of nothing but his pigs." Exasperation fought with humor in her voice, but, suddenly, her eyes widened and she stared at nothing over the rim of the glass she'd just raised to her lips. She lowered it slowly.

"What is it, Miss Morgan?"

"You *can't* be correct. My aunt cannot be such a goose."

"I am, and she can. But that doesn't account for your expression."

"My aunt, Lord John, suggested to us—after one of her diatribes—that I help Lord Brookhaven compose his maiden speech in the Lords."

Lord John's shout of laughter drew eyes. "She *didn't*."

"I find it insulting that you think I'd be no help to him."

Lord John ceased laughing at her militant look, but a twitch to one side of his mouth indicated he'd only suppressed his humor. "You misunderstood, Phill . . ." He waited a fraction of an instant but received no encouragement to use her name. ". . . I mean, Miss Morgan. It is not that you could not help, but that she used such excellent tactics. Her expertise touched my admittedly wry sense of humor. She is a formidable general, is she not?"

Phillida shook her head. "I don't understand."

"You agreed to her suggestion, did you not?"

Phillida's reply was slow: "I asked Lord Brookhaven if he wished my help." His lordship's brow quirked interrogatively. Phillida threw him a rueful glance. "He said he didn't wish to give a speech at all, but if it was necessary he do something so ridiculous, then someone must write the thing entirely—not just help."

"Which you will do?"

"Which I offered to do." She sighed. "An error, I see, but since I *have* offered I see no way of withdrawing."

"No, that would be dishonorable. Worse, it would lead Lady Brookhaven to try a new ploy. Put it off as long as you may while I draw his lordship off."

"How may you do that?" Phillida tipped her head, eyeing Lord John with a speculative gleam. "He appears to have no interest in the sporting life, and I don't believe him to be in the petticoat line, and . . ." She frowned. "Now what have I said to make you look like thunder? My mention of petticoat company? But I am more than seven." His scowl deepened. "Is it so bad of me?"

"Ignoring the impropriety of speaking cant you should not know, do you see me as a totally useless fribble, spending all my time at play?"

"Well, since you ask . . ."

"Did I say you tended to teach me salutary lessons, m'dear?" There was an ominous note to his voice. "You, Miss Morgan, will drive me to extremity."

Phillida chuckled. "Give over. You'd not put a gun to your head."

"Did I suggest such a thing?"

"Did you not?"

"No. I've a far better plan. I shall strangle *you.*"

They laughed, and Mr. Merryweather, one of London's more notorious gossips, eased nearer, hoping to discover what amused Lord John so thoroughly.

"You haven't clarified what you will do about my problem, my friend."

"Wait and see, my dear. I'll take him in hand as soon as I can. Perhaps I may begin now."

Phillida turned. "Oh, dear. I had hoped . . ." She bit her lip, her eyes flying to his. "Now stop that. It isn't kind to laugh at me," she scolded.

Lady Brookhaven sailed up to them. "Phillida, you are a severe disappointment to me. I must have a talk with you when we return home—which we are about to do. Osbourn!"

The young man jumped guiltily away from the punch bowl where he'd been reaching for a fruit cup. "Yes, Grandmother?"

"Go fetch our coach. We leave at once."

One last longing look at the punch and Lord Brookhaven turned away. Lord John sighed. "I erred, Miss Morgan." Lady Brookhaven, about to make an abrupt departure, was stunned by such an admission and awaited his explanation. "I said I'd begin this evening?" Phillida nodded. "It must wait. Tomorrow, then. We'll take our drive as usual?"

Phillida resisted her aunt's insistent hand. "A trifle earlier? Half past ten?"

Lord John closed his eyes in pretended pain. "There is no mistaking you are a green miss from the country, Miss Morgan. Half past ten, indeed. Why, that is the middle of the night!"

"Is it, my lord?" she asked with pretended demureness. "Then I fear our drive must be postponed. I shall be busy the rest of the day."

Merryweather boggled. Not only did this pert miss scold the biggest catch on the marriage mart, she turned down his company when offered it. It wasn't to be believed.

"In that case, although it will be a severe strain on my system, I will arrive promptly at half-ten." He bent a stern look her way. "I'd expect you to be waiting, Miss Morgan."

"Do you?"

He grinned. "Minx"

Lady Brookhaven gnashed her false teeth at the easy manners between the pair and swept her niece away from a man she now considered her enemy.

Five

Wagering on a marriage between Lord John and Miss Morgan became the newest rage. The odds swung wildly—especially when no one could make heads or tails of Merryweather's latest *on dit* concerning the not-so-young miss from the country and Society's most eligible lord.

Considering that women were protected from such business, the fact that Miss Morgan heard nothing of the controversy was unsurprising. What amazed his friends was that Lord John appeared equally unaware of the stir. Their assumption was incorrect. Lord John knew exactly what was in the wind. In private he either laughed or snarled—depending on his mood of the moment.

Lady Brookhaven was also unaware of the betting amongst the *goes*. She was merely pleased that, no sooner did her grandson arrive in London than there was a falling off of the attentions of the men she'd chosen as foils for him. It didn't occur to her that Miss Morgan's suitors were not put off by Osbourn, but that not one had the least delusion he could compete against Lord John. They thought it very bad of his lordship to toy with the lady's affections when they might, otherwise, win her for themselves.

Tuttles received word that Lady John would not immediately remove from Cambridgeshire. Independently he and Lord John heaved sighs of relief. The latter went with lighter heart to collect Miss Morgan for their morning drive. Both were quiet, thinking their separate thoughts, until they reached the Park, where Lord John mused: "I do not understand how it is, Phil—er . . ." He glanced at her and discovered her head was bent over her fingers. Why didn't she say something? "Miss Morgan? Are you attending?"

"It would be excessively impolite to do otherwise, would it not?"

"To say nothing of further denting my self-esteem, which is already damaged very nearly beyond repair."

He caught a glimpse of laughing eyes when she glanced around the brim of her bonnet. They were, he thought, very nice eyes. Especially when she laughed. If only she weren't, more often than not, laughing at him! "As I began to say," he said, "I can't understand why my mother and I never agree."

Phillida had been blessed by Flint with a verbal portrait of Lady John as an overbearing witch who could not keep her nose from other people's business. Even if the faults had been exaggerated, they should be obvious to someone as perspicacious as Lord John. Could he really be that blind?

"Have you no words of wisdom for me, Ph—hmm, I mean *Miss Morgan?*" Why did she not ask him to use her name? Any other woman would have done so the *first* time he pretended to slip. "My pardon, Miss Morgan. Could you repeat that?"

Phillida chuckled. "It is most rude to ask advice and not attend, my lord," she teased.

"Will you please cease milording me?" Lord John remembered that Phillida was not up to snuff. If he were to get their friendship on a more informal basis, he would simply have to ask that it be so. Besides, it was more and more difficult to remember to call her Miss Morgan when he always thought of her as Philly. He glanced at her and nearly chuckled at her shocked expression. "We've become friends, have we not?" he coaxed. "Such good friends that perhaps we might begin to use each other's name?"

Phillida hesitated. "Certainly we may—when alone, my lord, but I fear it might mislead people into thinking we've a decided partiality for each other if it were known by others that we do so."

"But we do have a decided partiality. At least, I do . . . Phillida."

Instantly her heartbeat increased unbearably. She searched, but found none of the softness one should see in a lover's gaze—only that twinkle which so often met her own laughing look. Ah. He was jesting. Her hands gripped each other tightly, but she gave no other sign of the sudden discovery that she'd done a most unwise thing: Phillida Morgan, spinster, had fallen in love with a rogue who avoided all thought of marriage and who, in any case, preferred blonds.

"Phillida?"

"What? Oh. I'm sorry. My mind was miles away. What were we . . . Oh yes, I remember." She raised startled eyes to Lord John's. "Do you know, I haven't a notion what name to call you—since we've agreed on Christian names, my lord!"

Lord John blinked. "Have we agreed? I'm delighted it is so." But he worried at the problem of a woman who was so unaware of him she didn't know his name. "Phillida, how can you not . . . Of course. We were informally introduced, were we not?" He puffed up his chest and intoned in a pompous way, "Dear lady, I wish you will be kind to my friend, Lucas Strathedene, Earl John and Baron Strathe. Please him very much by being so generous with your favors as to call him Lucas."

Phillida, putting aside her newly acquired self-knowledge, forced a merry laugh. "I love it when you are funning. So few people understand what it is to banter and joke and lightly tease. I don't know how I'll survive when I must return to Briarton and will no longer have you as a friend—Lucas."

"But you aren't to return to Briarton, are you?"

Between the harassment she was enduring at Brookhaven House and her sudden awareness of strong but unwanted feelings for Lord John, perhaps that was just what she wished to do. "Yes, my lo . . . Lucas, I believe I must."

"No, no. You cannot take away my new friend." He waved a hand airily. "It's unthinkable."

She smiled as she knew he intended. "I will not obey Lady Brookhaven's demand that I induce poor Osbourn to offer for me. Since I won't, I believe it behooves me to take myself home. If she invited me for that purpose only, and I believe you're correct about that, it is surely rude to continue to accept her hospitality while having no intention of fulfilling her wishes."

Lord John recognized the serious nature of her suggestion. It wasn't, he supposed, quite honorable to stay under a roof where you were in opposition to the wishes of your hostess. On the other hand, he truly did *not* want her to go. The notion was excessively distressing.

"Phillida," he said, choosing his words with care, "she didn't suggest any such thing in her invitation, did she? Therefore, you accepted in good faith, is that not correct? And therefore, one may conclude, you should continue as you have begun. Besides," he added, "how are we to find you a husband if you do *not?* And another thing, my dear. Just a *little* thing, of course." He grinned at her when she gave him a wary look. "Don't look so suspiciously. It's simply that I wish you to stay here where we may continue our delightful friendship. Phillida . . ."

"Yes?"

"Phillida, I wish you to know I like you very much indeed. It isn't what romantics call a *decided partiality,* but I'd miss you if you were to return to the obscurity of the village from whence you came."

"Thank you, my lor . . . er, Lucas." There was a decided break in her voice and she cleared her throat.

"Is it so difficult to call me by my name?"

There was a faintly wistful note to that, and Phillida searched his profile for a clue as to why. She wished she might ask that he return her home, but to do so would be impolite. How was she to act naturally, knowing what she now knew about her emotions? And his. Could love mix with friendship? Perhaps she could pretend to be ill?

He sighed. "I see it is."

"My lord? I mean, Lucas?"

"And thus you prove it." He slowed his team and turned slightly to study her. She had, he thought, a very nice profile, lovely clean lines to jaw and forehead and delightfully tempting lips, a small straight nose which, ever so slightly, turned up at the tip and hair which was always clean and heavy and tempting him to touch it. . . . And then there was the rest of her. . . .

"Why do you look at me in that manner?"

"Like how, Philly?"

She frowned. "Now, that I *did not* agree to. I dislike of all things to have my name shortened in such a way. Why are you staring at me?"

"Why?" Why was he staring? Why, because it had suddenly become clear how much he would miss her were she gone—her tender heart, intelligent mind, sense of humor. Why stare? Because it was clear she was just the woman for whom he'd given up searching! And, of all things, she was the one woman he'd ever met who did not attempt to—accidentally of course—fall into his arms or scheme and beg for his attentions! This was terrible.

"Lucas, are you all right?" Had she, she wondered, given him some clue to the depth of her feelings? He'd hate that. He might even cease to show her any favor at all—let alone such distinguishing attentions. And that, thought Phillida, would be unbearable.

"Philly, would you mind very much if I curtailed today's drive? I have just remembered a long-standing engagement with an old friend who is . . . er . . . who is in town only briefly, and, although I am perfectly willing to forget it all over again, I think I should not."

Phillida hid a sigh which combined relief he'd take her home and fear he'd just begun a program of withdrawal. "I think it a very good idea, Lucas." She used his name defiantly: if she were soon to lose his company forever, she would take every opportunity to voice the name she knew would always be dear to her.

"It is?"

Phillida scrambled to remember what she'd just said. She raised a hand to her forehead. "I seem to have a megrim this morning, Lucas. I fear I am very poor company indeed. I can't seem to keep my mind on our conversation for the ache."

"Ah, that explains it."

"Explains what, Lucas?"

"Explains why your attention wandered more than usual. Perhaps you'll be feeling more the thing tomorrow and will only give me one or two set-downs instead of one right after another?"

She chuckled, relieved she would have at least one more drive with him. "You are bamming me again. It is too bad of you when you've just been told I am feeling not quite the thing."

"Hmmm. Do you think you'll attend Lady Cowper's breakfast tomorrow? I'll not ask if you are to be at the Pepperling ball tonight. You will not wish to attend if you are feeling down-pin."

"I doubt I'll be allowed the indulgence of refusing, Lucas. My aunt allows no one but herself to fall ill. Admittedly, she herself indulges in an ailment only on the rarest of occasions—most usually when there is something she prefers not to do," she said as he pulled up before the Brookhaven town house.

Lord John came around the back of the carriage and reached to lift her down. "If you'll be there, I'll not avoid the ball. I'll see you tonight, Phillida."

"Very good, *my lord.*" She turned her eyes sideways, then rolled them up.

Lord John, noting who stood nearby with ears on the prick, chuckled. "Ah, what I meant to say was, good day, *Miss Morgan.*" Lord John lifted her hand and turned it, pressing his lips to her wrist where blue veins showed above short gloves and below the narrow ruffle at the end of her sleeve. He straightened slowly, his eyes not leaving hers.

Phillida blushed, glowered, and stalked up the steps to the door Lady Brookhaven's footman held open. She looked back, perplexed, and was surprised to find him staring at her. Lord John bowed. She dropped a brief, very nearly insulting curtsy, turned and entered the house with an indignant flick of her skirts. How dare he put on that charade? That the awful Merryweather had observed the whole was *terrible.* Had Lord John— *Lucas*—played up for the old gossip's benefit?—or had there truly been a new warmth in his gaze?—or was she indulging in wishful thinking, seeing what she wished to see?—or was it only that her head ached so much that nothing made the least sense?

Phillida went to her room in opposition to her greataunt's order to join her and Osbourn in the drawing room, pausing only long enough to ask the butler to tell her aunt she was suffering from a megrim of grim proportions and that if she were to attend the ball this evening she must rest.

Lady Brookhaven received this news far more calmly than the butler had girded himself to expect. Her ladyship was not disabused of the soothing notion Lord John had given her stubborn niece a long expected set-down until that evening—nor of the equally wrongheaded conviction that her formally intractable niece would, from now on, be more docile.

"Yes, Lady John postponed her visit. My lady discovered a plot in the parish to undermine her control of the vicar, who, at the moment, is in her pocket. She won't leave the field of battle until she secures her position," explained Tuttles. "What have you done while I've slaved in vain?"

Porterman accepted the offered pewter mug. "I've took up with Sir Romney's valet. He's greener than grass and tries not to show how shocking he finds the gossip I tell him. It's as good as a play to watch him swallow and look knowing and say as how it's just like Lord Whoever or Lady Someone Else to act *so*. My friend, I haven't had so much fun in years."

Tuttles breathed a prayer of thankfulness. If nothing else came out of their plotting, his friend had found new joy in life. "Why do you do it?"

"To bring Sir Romney back together with his first love, of course." Porterman took a long draft. "If I can. My, that's good ale." He smacked his lips. "One of my tales was about how a certain young lady wore the willow and never married," he said slyly. "Perhaps Sir Romney will take a quick jaunt to Tunbridge Wells?" He noted his daughter's deep scowl and angry approach and ducked his head, hiding, inadequately, behind his tankard.

"Mr. Tuttles," she said, "I wish to know what your precious master has done to my mistress. You are to tell me *immediately*. At once, I say." Mrs. Flint's flashing eyes, the fists doubled into her generous hips, the forethrust chin, all revealed barely pent anger and distress.

"Sit you down, missus," said Tuttles soothingly. "I haven't a notion of what you speak. If you'll explain, perhaps we can find a solution to your problem. You say something is wrong with Miss Morgan?"

"She went driving with the rogue this morning and came home moped. A megrim, she said, the back of her hand to her forehead. Some headache! It stands near six foot and weighs thirteen stone or so."

Tuttles frowned. "Are you saying they quarreled? But Lord John is in high jig, almost his old self. Not once recently has he fallen into the dismals." Tuttles narrowed his eyes thoughtfully. "*Occasionally* he goes very quiet, his eyes out of focus, and he frowns"—his aspect lightened—"but then he *chuckles*. Besides, he's eating better. I thought when I served him breakfast he'd fallen in love and, soon, we'd have a proper mistress again."

"Fallen in love? Bah. If he loved her, my miss would not be mumbling about how she doesn't belong in London and how she misses her mother and how she might as well do as Lady Brookhaven wants and marry Lord Brookhaven and then she sent me away on an errand so she may cry."

"It sounds simple enough to me," Porterman interrupted.

"Then, Father, you just explain it in simple words, because I don't know if I'm on my head or my heels for the worry."

"I'd guess your miss discovered she's head over heels in love with Lord John, but don't know he's in love with her. And being a modest sort of girl with a sensible head on her shoulders, she is certain he never *will* love her.

Of course she's suffering a megrim or two or three. Anyone would."

"Why shouldn't he love her!"

"Now don't bristle like a hedgehog, daughter. If you don't remind me of your sainted mother when you do that!"

Mrs. Flint remembered how her mother's temper could send her father running for cover. "I apologize, Father, for reminding you of Mother, but I ask again, what is wrong with my miss that Lord John wouldn't love her?"

"Now don't be silly, woman." Tuttles allowed his irritation to show. "It's obvious. Think of the women Lord John has favored. Diamonds, one and all. Tall, long pale hair, heavy-lidded eyes—and last, but most certainly not least, they are placid if not outright somnolent! Your miss is nice enough to look at, but dark and only average tall. Nor, you'll admit, is the dew still on her. She knows it if you don't. Furthermore, if you think Miss Morgan a calm and retiring miss, then I'm mistaken in your intelligence."

"Yes," said Porterman, "she's older than a proper bit he might be expected in the usual way to choose for a wife, but she's *not* an old married lady with no grass growing on her and aware where a flirtation may lead. So she treats him like a friend, and *he* don't know *her* feelings."

Tuttles agreed and added, "What your young lady don't know is that Lord John is very likely drawn to just that."

"Mere friendship?" Flint sneered.

"Don't you be thick now. It don't suit you. What I mean is that he admires the fact she don't toad-eat him. He's animadverted on the fact she is rude enough to think of something other than himself when they are together and that she lets her mind wander when he's speaking to her."

"I see. His pride is pricked. *He* isn't in love. But he's very likely determined to make my miss fall in love with him, and then he'll let her down hard for revenge. I don't like it." Flint shook her head. "Not at all."

"Now, daughter, don't go jumping fences you've not got to. I think her lack of proper respect may very well have drawn Lord John's attention first off, but I think it very likely he's discovered her good points by now and has taken the tumble into Cupid's game-pouch."

"How poetic. I think." Mrs. Flint stared at her father. "Or do you mean . . ."

Porterman's cheeks reddened. "Now daughter! I meant no disrespect. 'Tis only a phrase I once heard. Now give over that glaring and let's fix on a way to help our lovers to a proper conclusion."

They'd not more than put their heads together than a footman in livery rushed in and handed Tuttles a note. The butler closed his eyes in a pained way after reading it, drew in a deep breath, and let it out slowly.

"Trouble, old friend?"

"Yes, and her name is Lady John. She discovered a solution to her little problem." Tuttles paused dramatically. "She's bringing the vicar with her—a treat for the poor man, she says."

Early the next morning, Lord John was in no better humor than the rest of his household. His campaign to win his love was arduous enough without his interfering mother on his hands. While planning ways of dealing with his mother, Lord John paid too little attention to his horses. It took twenty minutes to soothe the ruffled sensibilities of the owner of an overturned wagon, to cheer with generous recompense the flower woman who lost her blooms to the gutter and to reply in properly ribald fashion to an early-rising friend's joshing for having caused the tangle in the first place. On top of that, his appointment with Weston dragged on when they argued over the size of buttons for his new vests.

Finally arriving for his drive with Phillida, he found the butler more starched up than usual. "I said," repeated Lord John, "please give Miss Morgan a message: Although late, I have arrived for our drive."

"Miss Morgan is not at home," the butler reiterated.

Lord John flipped open his watch. "She hadn't the courtesy to wait a mere half an hour?"

"M'lord?"

Lord John felt his cheeks heat. Surely he hadn't asked that question of Lady Brookhaven's butler? But he had. "Can you tell me where Miss Morgan is to be found?" He tossed a guinea and caught it, tossed it again.

The butler glanced over his shoulder into the hall and, leaning forward, both ways along the street, he quickly mumbled, "Lady Brookhaven dragged Miss Morgan off to look at the new patterns at Wedgwood and Byerley's showroom in York Street."

"Now why is Lady Brookhaven patronizing such a place?"

Again the butler looked from right to left and over his shoulder. "She was heard to say, m'lord, that perhaps shopping for household things would put Miss Morgan into a proper frame of mind. She is planning on taking her to the linen shops in Oxford Street tomorrow."

Lord John chuckled as he slipped the yellow boy into the butler's practiced hand. "How interesting. And who knows? Perhaps such shopping *will* put Miss Morgan in a mind to think of marriage."

Although it seemed an age, he soon pulled up near the shop's entrance. He chose a boy to hold his horses and entered the huge, well-lighted room. Tall windows along the side let in the sun, which shone off the hand-painted china and the glass-enclosed cases protecting the best pieces. He strolled between the tables and pillars in search of his love.

His love was moping.

Lady Brookhaven scowled. "Phillida, I will not put up with such a sour face. Now which of these two patterns do you like best?"

"I don't particularly like either, Aunt Em. I don't wish to purchase a set of dishes. In fact, I have no wish to buy anything at all." She glanced around the showroom. "Haven't you seen enough, Aunt Emily?"

"Do refrain from whining, missy. I'll not have it. Simply because you are forced to admit what has been obvious to everyone else for some time is no reason to make an exhibition of yourself."

"What is it that has been so obvious, Aunt Em?"

"Why, that Lord John is bored to tears with bear-leading you and that he's done with you."

"I believe, my lady," a deep voice spoke over Lady Brookhaven's shoulder, "you should determine the facts of the case before you attempt to refine upon them. Good morning, Phillida. I was very sorry to be delayed this morning."

"Lord John! How did you find—er—I mean, good morning, my lord." Lady Brookhaven held out two fingers which he just touched with the tips of his own. "Now, if you'll excuse us, we've finished here and must go at once to an appointment at our glovers." She made shooing movements toward Phillida which her niece ignored. "A tedious hour or two," she gushed, "but if one wishes gloves to fit properly, one must endure the time it takes to measure each finger and thumb."

"Aunt, I believe you've mistaken the date. Our appointment at the glovers is tomorrow." Phillida ignored her aunt's attempt to speak. "I, too, was sorry to miss our ride this morning, Lord John," she said.

Lord John also ignored Lady Brookhaven. "If you've completed your errands, why may we not indulge ourselves now?" Lord John offered an arm to each lady. Phillida smiled a grateful smile and placed her fingers on his right arm. Lady Brookhaven, gracelessly, took the other. He saw Lady Brookhaven into her carriage, retaining hold of Phillida as he did so.

Lord John grinned wolfishly. "Wedgwood and Byerley have a very stimulating display, do they not? *Most* inspiring."

Lady Brookhaven managed to insert a caveat. "You have done no shopping, my lord. My niece should come with me so you may finish it."

"I came for just one perfect item. Believe me, I found it," he said with a straight face and only a glance at Phillida. "I will bring Miss Morgan home in good time to ready herself for the Cowpers' breakfast."

Knowing herself beaten, Lady Brookhaven nodded and sat back. The door to the carriage was closed and, when the footman had jumped up behind, it started forward.

Lord John spoke very little until he and Phillida reached their favorite drive in the Park. "I didn't expect to get you away from Lady Brookhaven so smoothly, Phillida." He glanced at her when she didn't respond with expected congratulations and exclamations. He grinned to himself that he'd thought she might do anything so trite. "Did she fill your ears all morning with stupid notions such as I overheard?" he asked.

"Yes. But she could have saved her breath. I'd already begun to wonder if you weren't tired of taking me around."

"I thought we'd been through all that. Didn't you believe me when I said I'd miss you if you were to leave London?"

"We could meet at the various entertainments, my lord. You needn't make an extra effort to see me, such as this drive."

"Ah. I was afraid you'd misunderstand."

"Misunderstand, my lord?"

"Phillida, why are you milording me again?"

"I presume you've had second thoughts and changed your mind, that I was not to pursue the familiarity we agreed to yesterday—since you didn't come at the usual hour for our drive."

"What it is to have a reputation for punctuality. I see I must describe how I embarrassed myself this morning . . ." He soon had her chuckling as he outlined his part in the morning's contretemps. "Ham-handed!" he admitted, shaking his head. "The merest whipster would have done better."

"That's a plumper."

"Even the best of drivers errs if he, foolishly, thinks of something else just when he should pay attention to his horses."

"And were you thinking of something else?" Phillida bit her lip, looking sideways at him around the corner of her bonnet. How had she dared to ask such an impertinent and leading question!

Lord John considered telling her that it was she that had been on his mind. He did a quick calculation, decided it was too soon to admit she was driving him to distraction, and said, "I learned just before I left the house for Weston's—where I ordered two coats and three new waistcoats—that my mother arrives soon, after all. It's enough to put the most saintly of men in a furor—and I make no claims to sainthood."

"Why will you find a visit from her so distressing?"

she asked, wishing his excuse had been herself, but unsurprised when it wasn't.

"She will nag and shrew and harangue until I wish her to the devil."

"She is a prattle-box? Can't you hire your mother a companion and pay her to listen? Pay her *well* to listen? Or perhaps find a slightly deaf old lady who will not mind if she chatters on and on?"

Lord John chuckled. "I love your sense of humor, Philly. The thing is," he went on before she could once again object to the pet name, "it's only me at whom she nags. As long as my brother lived she ignored me, but now she'll have some new and ineligible female—from my point of view—to puff off as an appropriate bride. I'll not be caught as my brother was, but I'll need all my ingenuity to avoid the traps she'll set. At the same time I must avoid hurting the lady who will have been primed to receive my addresses." He sighed. "I wish I might avoid going through it all again. We play out the same farce each time we are both in Town."

"I understand exactly what you mean. I am getting that sort of nagging from my aunt. Her grandson, she says, would be the perfect mate. I believe she thinks I may mother him for the next thirty or forty years along with whatever babes we produce and see that the *next* heir to the earldom isn't a mooncalf who can see no further than the inside of a pigsty."

"She's begun her campaign at a more obvious level, has she?"

"Yes. It is tedious to be polite in the face of her endless cajolery when she knows it will not do. Poor Osbourn. He is about to make me an offer simply to make her be still—he's holding out only because he's not *yet* convinced I'll say no."

"He is a mooncalf, is he not? Why would you be tempted to say yes?"

"It is supposed I should be tempted for all those things a woman is believed to want, but most of all, for security. He forgets I have that."

"Do you?"

His tone had an edge to it, and she glanced at him, discovering his eyes had narrowed slightly and his brows drawn together. "Yes. My grandmother left me a tidy fortune. Oh, nothing the ton would consider excessive, but an adequate competence. I need not marry a callow boy such as Osbourn merely to ensure I continue living as I've always done—something many girls *must* do." In the middle of the explanation Phillida felt Lord John relax and wondered why he'd reacted so strangely. She thought over what she'd said, and her spine stiffened to rigidity. She glared at him. "How dare you!"

"Hmmm? How dare I what, Philly love?"

She ignored his use of the despised nickname in favor of the higher priority of his insult to her. "How dare you think me so certain of your regard I consider you a source of future support? How *could* you?"

"Phillida, I reacted instinctively." When her lips only tightened, he added, "Think of all those girls you referred to who must find a husband or be dependent on relatives for their very food. Any one of them, given the attention I've paid you, would have concluded I was courting her and would only be waiting, breathlessly, for the opportunity to say yes."

Phillida thought about that and gradually relaxed. "I apologize."

"So do I for giving you the need to apologize. I *should* have known better, Phillida. I *do* know you better. In fact," he said, inspiration striking, "I know you so well, I am about to ask a really Gothic favor of you." He frowned, gazing into the middle distance.

"Yes, Lucas?" she encouraged.

"Phillida, allow me to explain the whole of it before

you object." He still didn't look at her. "Please? I don't want you throwing hammers in the spokes before you hear me out." His brows flew up and down in a decidedly clownish fashion, and Phillida chuckled. "To begin, you are suffering from Lady Brookhaven's attempt to marry you off to her cloddish grandson. True?"

"Yes—but he isn't so cloddish as all that. He is merely a simple man who has no interest in Society and doesn't pretend to be other than he is—for which I admire him—but *not*," she hurried to add, "enough to wed him."

"Never mind that. You suffer now and, soon, I'll suffer, correct?"

"I'm listening." She clenched her hands, guessing what he had in mind.

"Isn't it obvious? If we pretend to an engagement— agreeing to break it off whenever either of us wishes to—then my mother and your aunt could no longer torture us with their demands. We'd have spiked their guns!"

Phillida fought with her baser self before asking, "Don't you fear, if we do as you suggest, that some circumstance might force you, in the end, to actually marry me?"

"Formal engagements are not to be broken lightly. We both know that." He searched his mind for a solution, didn't like what he came up with, but it was the best he could do. "I'll guarantee to give you proper reason to do so at whatever point in our charade you decide we must break it off."

"How might you do that?"

"In a variety of ways. I might, for instance, flirt in an obvious and very public way with some fashionable lady well known for being not quite the thing, and do it where you would catch me out. Your righteous anger will be commended by the ton, and I, the villain, will be formally booed just as villains are supposed to be."

Phillida ignored his humor. "You will tell me when you wish to break it off? You will not let me find it out in a way, such as you've just described, with no previous warning?"

"Phillida, we must agree to be honest with each other," said Lord John, adding a silent caveat to the effect that total honesty must wait until he'd taught her to love him. "I will not hesitate to tell you if my eye lights on some new woman I feel I cannot live without." Lord John knew he was safe in making that promise. He went on with a touch of strain. "You will be equally frank with me, of course. Will our little plot serve?"

Phillida bit her lip. To be engaged to Lord John as a prank would be very nearly more than she could bear. Wouldn't it?

"Phillida?"

If she were to agree, wouldn't her feelings only deepen unbearably? Wouldn't it make future suffering *worse?* Or might a sham engagement provide her with memories she could treasure in a future which was bound to be lonely? As things stood now she must hide her every desire to touch him, or to smile at him lovingly or to speak an endearment. If they were engaged—even a pretend engagement—she could allow expression to any or all such urges, and he, dear sweet man, would only think it good acting on her part. Which settled it. . . . Didn't it?

"Phillida, if you do not care for the notion . . ."

Which *would* be the better part of valor? To say no and leave town. . . ? Or to say yes and no longer fear accidental exposure of her feelings for him? And, besides that, have a glorious time, making memories to lighten what she foresaw would be a very dull future?

"My dear, I didn't mean to put you into a quandary. Is

it so difficult for you to tell me yes or no? Would you like more time to think on this?"

Phillida, coming out of her brown study, blinked at him. "Did you say something, my lord? I was thinking, you see."

He smiled wryly. "It was nothing. Has your thinking helped you to a decision? Will you honor me by trusting me enough to say yes?"

"I will."

"I'll send the notice in immediately."

They, both of them, secretly heaved a sigh of profound relief.

Lucas had managed to mark her, in the eyes of the ton at least, as his own. Poachers would be prosecuted and transported far away from her!

Phillida had found a much more satisfactory solution to the problem of loving Lucas than the only other she'd been able to discover. It would *not* be necessary to leave London—leave *him*—and, on some pretext, return home.

Each of them smiled satisfied little smiles which were noted by that great gossip Merryweather. He immediately hurried off to lay a bet on the side of a marriage between the couple, wishing to get it down before an interesting announcement made it ineligible to place another bet. It was too bad he must leave town just now when things were so interesting. Such a bore, business, when he could be amongst the ton who were life and breath itself to him. Merryweather sighed hugely. Well, it was only for a day or two. . . .

Six

Lady Brookhaven turned her head first one way and then the other, back and forth, catching her wig occasionally when it slipped to one side. "Phillida," she said, when she could stand it no more, "you have been unlike yourself ever since you came into the breakfast room more than an hour ago. *Then* you played with your eggs and ham, which you never do. *Now* you are uncommonly unable to settle, and you pace my salon carpet until I fear you'll wear holes in it. Sit yourself down," she ordered.

"I'm sorry, Aunt." Phillida walked toward the indicated chair, but changed direction before reaching it and headed for the windows, only to turn again and head for the door when Lady Brookhaven's butler, Greyson, announced Lord John. They met in the middle of the room, and she clung to the hands he held out.

"What's the matter, m'love?" he asked softly.

"I think we've done the wrong thing," she whispered. "Can we talk?"

"Cold feet?" His brows rose, but his smile was kind. "If you're wishing to change your mind, m'dear, I fear it's too late." He placed her hand on his arm and they strolled toward Lady Brookhaven, who watched them approach, with a sour look on her face. "My lady," announced Lord John, "we wish you to be among the first to know we are engaged to be married."

"Impossible. You can't be engaged."

Lord John's brow arced. "There is no impediment, of which I know."

"Phillida, you're a fool." Lady Brookhaven rose majestically to her feet, glaring at her great-niece and the tall man hovering possessively near her. "Not that it matters," she said complacently, with the gummy smile Phillida hated. "You're too late. As you'll see, there is an impediment." She strode to the tapestry bellpull hanging by the fireplace and yanked it so viciously that the tassel came off. Glancing at it, she harrumphed and threw it to the floor, then strode back to the pair watching her, Lord John with interest and Phillida warily.

The butler entered. "You rang, my lady?"

"Have this morning's papers arrived?" The butler bowed, saying they had. "Well, dolt? Bring them. At once."

"Yes. Do," said Lord John. "I didn't read the announcements before leaving home this morning."

"The annou . . ." Lady Brookhaven's hand went to her throat in an out-of-character movement of distress. "The . . ." She reached behind her for a chair, sat down with a thump. "Lord John, are you intimating you've *already* inserted a notice of this . . . this engagement?"

"I sent it in yesterday."

Lady Brookhaven laughed. She chuckled. The chuckles turned wild.

Her laughter continued as she lolled back in her chair, uncontrollable, the tears rolling down her cheeks. Phillida and Lord John stared at each other. He shrugged. "You do it," he decided. "She's your aunt."

Phillida sighed. "Excuse me, Aunt Em," she said politely. The sound of a sharp slap against rouged cheek seemed overly loud to the young woman.

For a moment Lady Brookhaven stared in a bewildered fashion at her niece. Then, very quietly, she said, "Thank you."

"Aunt, whatever is the matter?"

"You'll see. Oh yes, *you'll* see."

Her ladyship straightened her back, reset her wig, and looked down at her feet. She waited, silently, for her butler's return. Phillida and Lord John again exchanged glances. He held out his hand and she moved back into the protection of his ambience, needing a sense of his presence to counteract the strangeness of her aunt.

The butler entered with the papers neatly folded and laid on a salver.

"Hmm. Yes, Greyson." She waved him away. "Put them on the table and be gone. I don't wish to be disturbed until further notice. I am not at home to *anyone*. I don't care what excuse is used by visitors, *I am not at home.*" She waited, staring into space, until the door closed. "I suggest you look over those announcements, my lord. We must determine what to do."

"Do, my lady?"

"Do, Aunt?"

"Are you hard of hearing?" She closed her eyes. "Oh, read the demned announcements!" In the distance the bell for the front door rang, and Lady Brookhaven grimaced. "Early as it is, it's begun. Thank the lord I had the wit to tell Greyson to deny me."

Again the pair exchanged glances. Lord John put an arm around Phillida's waist and led her to the table. Each reached for a newspaper. Each read the announcements in their paper and then exchanged it for the other.

Lord John turned to Lady Brookhaven. "What did you think to gain by inserting that notice, my lady?" he asked, his voice stern.

"The obvious. Phillida was marked for my grandson from the moment I met her. I invited her here for no other purpose than to promote a marriage between them. You, my lord, have been a thorn from the moment you took her up. Why," she asked querulously, "did you have to interfere?"

"Are you aware your niece planned to leave the delights of a London Season? That she intended to return to Briarton because she could not give in to your wishes that she marry your grandson?"

"She isn't such a fool. Give up a life as Lady Brookhaven when it is handed her on a salver? No. *You* are another matter entirely. I can see that catching *you* would be more than a wench could forgo." Lady Brookhaven's eyes narrowed. "I wonder if she believes she can hold you. With my grandson she'd never have a moment's worry."

"You would wish on her," responded Lord John when Phillida's hand tightened on his arm, "a lifetime of boredom."

"You don't deny the difficulty she'll have holding you," snarled Lady Brookhaven.

"Phillida knows how dearly I love her. It will be no fault in me if our marriage is not to her liking."

"Harrumph."

"Well, beloved?" Lucas looked to Phillida. His beloved was, once again, paying him no attention. "Phillida, m'dear," he said, "you are very quiet."

"I've been thinking what to do, but all that is in my mind is that my aunt has made me a laughingstock. My lord—Lucas, I cannot face the scandal which will begin the moment the ton reads their papers. Has any lady ever found herself in such a bumble-broth? I'm sure no one ever awoke to a new day and discovered herself formally betrothed at the same time to two peers of the realm!"

"How can you be so calm?" asked Lady Brookhaven. She'd considered succumbing—again—to hysterics, a condition she'd always considered the last resort of a foolish woman, but the current situation called for drastic measures, and the longer she thought of the probable complications, the more appealing she found a bout of hysterics. "I meant it for the best." Phillida looked her in disbelief. "I *did*. You'd be perfect for my grandson. You *would*," she repeated when Phillida shook her head.

"I would *not*. He needs a quiet little mouse of a woman who will think the sun rises and sets in him. He needs a woman who will give him one little Linwood after another. He needs someone he can guide and who will make him feel comfortable."

"That is just exactly what he mustn't have. Don't you see?" Lady Brookhaven evinced something very close to despair. "He will never play a proper role in the Party if that's the way of it!"

"He will never play the role you wish for him whomever he marries." Phillida reread the announcements. "Does Osbourn know about this?"

"Know about what, Cousin?" he asked, entering the room in time to hear her question. He sidled closer, glancing warily from his grandmother, who looked exceedingly nervous—an unusual situation, to say the least—to his cousin, who was trembling with ill-concealed anger.

"This."

Lord Brookhaven took the newspaper, read the notice to which she pointed, and paled to a dangerously ashen hue. He wavered, stumbled toward a chair—and didn't make it. Only Lord John's quick reflexes saved the young man from a fall. He helped Osbourn to a nearby sofa, sat him down, and pushed his head between his legs.

"I think that answers my question." Phillida stared at the old woman. "Lord Brookhaven knew no more of this announcement than I, did he? Well, Aunt?"

"I did it for the best."

"But without reference to our interests. You decided, with no regard for what would suit either of us, that *you* would be pleased by our union. What you refuse to see is that I would destroy your grandson. Worse, I would become a shrew—the worst sort of termagant. But you care not. You are a horrible, manipulating woman, Aunt." Phillida turned from Lady Brookhaven's gobbling to Lord John. His mouth was a stern line and his eyes cold and forbidding. "My lord," she said contritely, holding out her hand, which he took in one of his, "I fear I must use the prerogative of womankind and change my mind. I refuse your very kind offer to come to my . . ." His fingers touched her mouth, halting her flow of speech. After a searching look, she began again: "As I was saying, I must refuse your kind offer. I'll leave London as soon as my trunks are packed." His expression darkened and his grip on her hand increased to a painful degree. "Please forgive me."

"Forgive you, my dear? I've nothing to forgive *you*. I'm not certain I'll forgive your aunt. Her interference has caused me more pain than I may tell you. Will you not reconsider? We should face this thing together. Will you be so cruel"—he attempted a smile, but it was strained—"as to leave me to face the ton alone?" One eyebrow quirked interrogatively. Still holding her hand, he turned to Osbourn. "Lord Brookhaven, may we trust you to write a notice which will free Miss Morgan from this engagement into which you have *not* entered? One which will *not* set Miss Morgan up for ridicule?"

"Most happily, but . . . ," Osbourn gulped, "I don't know how to word it."

Lord John's lips twitched. "You shall come with me, Lord Brookhaven. We'll work on it together. . . . I was to attend a meeting of the Society of Agriculture this afternoon. Perhaps you, too, are a member?"

Phillida blinked. What was Lord John up to now?

"John Sinclair's Society?" Lord Brookhaven looked equally bewildered by the change of subject, but, ever polite, he answered, "No, my lord. I have wished to join ever since an acquaintance extolled its virtues, but have not yet put in for membership."

"I'll sponsor you. Sinclair has done an excellent thing, do you not agree, in forming an organization for the propagation of information concerning scientific farming. Sir Humphry Davy is lecturing today."

"Sir Humphry?" Osbourn's eyes lit up. "You'll take me?"

"My plans have changed, but I'll introduce you to someone who will."

Unable to insert a word, Lady Brookhaven's anger had grown. Now she managed it. "Enough!" she said. "You, Lord John, will stop encouraging Osbourn to join that stupid society. And I won't have Osbourn made the butt of jokes, so he'll write no notice. *You* will send in *your* denial of an engagement to my niece, Lord John, or I will . . ." For a moment she looked old and bewildered, then the look cleared. "I will blacken missy's name and your reputation. She will find yourself an outcast once I'm finished, and you, my fine lord, will be shunned by all right-thinking people."

"You forget, Lady Brookhaven," he said evenly, his eyes and his voice icy. "Phillida and I are to wed. My title will protect her."

Phillida tugged at his sleeve. This was what she'd most feared, predicting something would happen which would make him feel honor bound to marry her. "I will go home."

"You will do no such thing. I need you."

"You don't understand," she hissed.

"What don't I understand?" he asked patiently.

Phillida looked first at Lady Brookhaven and then toward Osbourn. She sighed. "You're not a fool. Don't let your temper make you one."

Lady Brookhaven's brows rose at the insult. They arched higher when Lord John's mood lightened just when one most expected it to become livid. What was between them? Obviously they knew one another a great deal better than she'd believed possible on such short acquaintance, despite his persistent pursuit. It was his persistence which had led her to insert her notice before it was too late. Except it was already too late . . . but how could she have known?

"I promise you I will never marry against my will, Philly," he said softly, patting her hand. "Is it that which bothers you?"

"But you must not marry out of pity, either."

"You are a delight, my love," he whispered, "but you worry needlessly. You'll see, love of my life." He bowed over her fingers.

"Don't come the toady, Lucas. Bowing and scraping and dishing out the butter don't suit you." She held back a laugh at his wry look. Shaking her head, she added, "Lucas, for the immediate future at least, I cannot face the ton. I must return home."

He considered the pricks and gibes and the heavy-handed joshing she'd endure when next she appeared in public. He, too, for that matter. "If you really wish to run away, Phillida, then, just as any gentleman should, I'll escort you." He laughed shortly. "Don't bite off my head, m'dear; I've a perfectly good reason for doing so. I, too, have no wish to face what the ton will dish out for the three of us. Besides, although you are of age and there is no legal need to ask for your hand, it is only polite to receive your mother's blessing. I wouldn't wish to be backward in doing the pretty."

Phillida met his eyes, read a warning there which she couldn't interpret. She gave up trying to tactfully bring him to acknowledge they'd been dropped into a bumble-broth which could only lead to disaster—or that his behavior was digging the trap deeper. She bit her lip, thinking, but for the moment was stymied. "I will pack. When may we leave?"

"Lord Brookhaven and I must write his retraction." Lord John frowned, playing with her fingers as he thought, behavior Phillida found exceedingly upsetting to her already precarious equilibrium. "I must introduce your cousin to someone who will take him to that lecture. . . . I foresee at least two hours before we may be gone. Can you be ready so quickly?"

"What is not ready may be sent later." Phillida glanced toward her great-aunt, who was slumped into the cushions of her couch. The woman looked old, but Phillida could feel no pity. The ploy to force herself and her cousin into marriage was despicable. "I will not thank you for a delightful holiday, Aunt," she said coldly. "Your manipulations have caused it to end on such a sour note that I may never remember the good things. Osbourn, I do not count our introduction among the bad. You were, as we both know, as much a dupe as I."

Her aunt glared. "I warn you, if you leave now, I will not let the insult pass lightly. I will set forward those rumors of which I spoke."

"Which," said Lord John calmly, "I will counter by querying your sanity. If I describe Lord Brookhaven's reaction when informed of his engagement, I think I will be believed, do you not?"

"I will not be thwarted."

The words were such as Phillida would expect of her aunt, but the woman looked ill and there was no force behind her words. Perhaps she *should* feel pity? "I believe you truly thought you were doing the best you could for your grandson, Aunt, but attempting to change a character which is fully formed is bound to lead to unhappiness. You must give up your ambitions to turn Osbourn into a political force. Instead, why not look about you for some young man to whom you could become patron? Some promising politician who hasn't the resources to make a noise for himself? Someone who would appreciate your help and advice?"

"My grandson must take his proper place in the Party."

"The party?" Osbourn rose hastily to his feet and blinked owlishly. *"Your* party? You mean the *Whigs?"*

"Of course, you nodcock. What other party could I mean?"

Osbourn's face was a picture of horror. "But, Grandmother, it is impossible." He paused, gulped, and then bravely explained: "I'm a Tory."

Lady Brookhaven fainted—whether from his politics or his presumption, no one could say.

Phillida clung to the strap, wondering why she'd assumed Lord John would ride beside the carriage the whole way. At their first change of horses he'd ordered Flint into the baggage carriage and entered this one. In such close company, how was she to hide from him the state of her emotions?

"Do you think me a terrible fool for running?" she asked.

"Phillida, if I thought you a fool, I'd never have proposed in the first place. Now we've been dumped into just such a difficulty as you foresaw and of which you warned me. Does that seem a reason for considering *you* a fool?"

"A coward, then."

"M'girl, it is unlike you to ask for compliments, and, since you ask, you won't get one. *Of course running is cowardly."* Phillida's eyes flashed at his response. He grinned and touched her nose. "But you're no more a coward than I! If you'd not decided to go home, I wonder what excuse I'd have found to take us out of London." He leaned against the squabs, his head turned her way, and mused. "A house party, perhaps? You and ten or twelve friends at my estate in Cambridgeshire while Mother is in Town? *Close* friends, of course, who would not tease us. It's my favorite residence, by the way."

"You would ask me to your country home when you've no hostess there?"

"Don't pretend shock that I'd enjoy finding you unchaperoned! You've more sense under your bonnet and must know how much I'd enjoy seducing you." Phillida gave him a withering look. She wasn't, she'd been assured, at all in his style. "Come to that, you'd enjoy it too," he added. He gently covered her mouth when she'd have chastised him. "I should not speak so to you. I'll behave. My aunt, who is nominally my mother's companion, never comes to London. She'd enjoy hostessing my hypothetical party. You'll like her, Philly, when you meet her. She's nothing like my mother."

The carriage bounced, bounced again, and Phillida, thrown toward him, reached for the strap she'd foolishly released. They were far beyond the cluster of rapidly growing villages around the old city of London. They'd even passed through some of the ten thousand acres devoted to vegetables for the city markets, and the four thousand of fruit—information she'd learned will-she nill-she from Osbourn. But, as they left the garden farms behind, the roads deteriorated and one soon became aware of the unavoidable aches and pains which, no matter how well sprung the carriage, one suffered.

Lord John watched his love's expressions. Now he said, "Phillida, you know it will be nothing more than a ten-day wonder, do you not? The notices of your engagement to two different men will raise eyebrows, but will not be a true scandal. There will be laughter at our expense, but by visiting your mother we'll avoid the worst of it."

"Lucas, you won't allow yourself to be forced to marry me, will you?"

"Is that *still* bothering you? Phillida, I promise, on my honor, to find a way out of this which will please the both of us. I will not allow myself to be forced into anything I do not want. You hurt my feelings that you continue, despite repeated reassurances, to believe otherwise." Again he turned his head against the squabs and noted she still frowned slightly. "Phillida, do you fear the reverse? That you might be forced to marry *me?*"

He held his breath only so long as it took for him to interpret the startled expression she turned his way. Such an idea had, very obviously, never crossed her mind.

"It isn't that," she admitted. "Only that I'd regret it for the rest of my life if I were the cause of your losing your chance for happiness."

"Now, there speaks the true friend." He relaxed. As long as she wasn't worried that wedding him would make her miserable, he'd time to convince her his *only* chance for happiness depended on their marriage. Again he turned to look at her. Blast. The frown still made a faint line between her beautiful eyes. "Phillida, love, something still troubles you?"

"Yes. It occurred to me I shouldn't have allowed Flint to ride in the second carriage. When you suggested it to her, I assumed you'd be riding. I like traveling alone. . . ." She glanced at him and blushed delightfully. "I didn't mean to say I object to your company, Lucas, but I just recalled it is improper in me to allow it."

"I wished to talk with you privately, Philly, since I'd

no chance to discover how overset you might be. Now that we've talked, I won't try your sensibilities. We stop soon for some tea and a change of horses. You may ask Flint to join us as chaperon when we take to the road for the last stage." His brows rose, querying her. "Knowing your nature, I must suppose you feared *you'd* compromise *me* if we were seen riding in a closed carriage together rather than the other way around. You must not worry. Nothing will happen which will make either of us unhappy. I've promised, remember?"

Phillida recalled that statement when, half an hour later, she allowed Sir John to hand her from the coach. Coming from the inn, a startled expression on his round face, was her nemesis, Mr. Merryweather. She raised her eyes in a dramatic way and sighed soulfully. Lord John, wondering why she was making a may-game of herself, looked around—and grinned. Turning back to her, he winked. "How," she asked with a politeness belied by clenched teeth, "can you find any amusement in this situation?"

"Such a multitude of errors makes it a comedy, Philly, m'love. Run along and find Flint. I think I'll invite His Wordiness to join us."

"You'll do no such thing!"

"You aren't thinking, m'love. How better to spread our side of the tale to the ton?" Lord John's eyebrows rose and fell and rose in a funny fashion.

Phillida, not really believing he'd invite Merryweather to join them, laughed, then feared it would turn into a fit of hysteria to match her aunt's exhibition of that morning. *Only* that morning? After freshening herself, she entered the private parlor entirely unsuspecting. It was in character with all else which had happened that day to find Mr. Merryweather ensconced near a blazing fire with a large glass of burgundy. Phillida turned an accusing look on Lord John, who stepped forward to place her hand on his arm.

"Mr. Merryweather," he said, "be among the first to wish my intended bride happy."

Merryweather rose to his feet and bowed. "Miss Morgan. Allow me to wish you very happy indeed. A sly puss you are to catch such a wary mouse in parson's trap, m'dear."

Phillida turned a disgusted look on Lucas, who grinned down at her. "I believe it is the other way around, Mr. Merryweather," she said. "I feel as if it is *I* who am trapped." She realized from the look on the old gossip's face that she'd said just the wrong thing, and added, "Such a delightful velvet-lined trap it is, but you must know that at my advanced age I'd no expectation of wedding anyone. Your surprise is nothing compared to my own, that I fell deeply in love—and so quickly, too. When one has my years in their cup, one gives up all notion of romance, believing it a fairy tale."

"I don't know why she keeps harping on her age." Lucas laughed. "I think her the perfect age for me, just as I am for her. I will never forget our first meeting. Will you, my love?"

Phillida remembered that momentous night when, escaping her boring suitors, she'd hoped for a few moments alone—only to discover a man who was anything but boring. A tiny smile played around her lips as some of their conversation ran through her mind. She blinked when Lucas touched her cheek with his fingertips. He smiled a knowing smile, and her expression faded as she realized what Mr. Merryweather would think of their little pantomime! After all, Lucas had *not* kissed her that night. In fact, he'd *never* kissed her. Not even that afternoon in the closed carriage when he'd had the perfect opportunity to do so. Ah, well. She already knew she wasn't the sort to whom Lucas paid such attentions. She pushed that distressing thought aside.

Lord John said, "You see, Merryweather, it was love at first sight, so it isn't surprising Lady Brookhaven panicked."

Phillida drew away from Lord John and went to stand before the fire, her back to the two men. She wanted nothing to do with Lord John's lies.

"Panicked, m'lord?" asked Merryweather, his avid curiosity roused. He looked from Lord John to the straight back of the lovely young woman.

"Yes. She had, she thought, arranged a marriage between her grandson and Phillida, but, silly woman, hadn't told either of them her plans. She'd wanted them to know each other first, you see. When she saw how well Philly and I dealt together, she sent an announcement to the papers concerning Miss Morgan and her grandson. Miss Morgan and I had just reached an agreement concerning our future, and I, too, sent in an announcement." Lord John heaved a sigh. "You can imagine the talk when *both* notices appeared in the same column. Most embarrassing. You can also imagine how glad we are we'd planned an immediate visit to Miss Morgan's mother and had a ready-made excuse to escape the ton's curiosity, which will be rampant."

"Both announcements appeared, m'lord?" Merryweather's eyes popped. "You mean to say Miss Morgan is engaged to you and to Lord Brookhaven, according to the announcements?"

"She is engaged only to me. Lord Brookhaven, on discovering what his grandmother had done, immediately wrote a retraction of any contract between himself and Miss Morgan. It will appear tomorrow."

"You say Lady Brookhaven sent in the announcement without discussing it with her grandson or Miss Morgan?"

"Yes. In her mind the arrangement was already made. But since neither Miss Morgan nor Lord Brookhaven had been consulted, we three agreed it was not a true contract." Lord John grinned. "Especially since neither Lord Brookhaven nor my lovely Phillida wished for the connection."

Phillida, surprised by how few lies were told, added, "If I'd known *why* my aunt asked me to come to London, I'd not have accepted her kind invitation. Lord Brookhaven is a worthy man, but he is not so old as I and we have no interests in common. We would not suit."

Merryweather nodded, a complicated combination of kind understanding and outright curiosity warping his expression oddly. He quaffed more wine while forming the shape of his next question. "How has your mother, Lady John, taken the news of your engagement, my lord?" he asked in plain English, having found no tactful way to probe for the answer to that interesting question.

"I haven't a notion, Merryweather. You are likely to discover it before I do. Mother arrives in Town soon, but we must do the pretty by Phillida's mother immediately. How lucky we are to leave behind the worst of the astonishment which will result from this mix-up."

Phillida had not formerly thought of Lady John and her likely reaction. She groaned softly, her eyes closing. Opening them, her bottom lip drawn between her fine teeth, she looked straight into Lucas's eyes and silently indicated her feelings on the subject. He smiled, shook his head slightly, and turned back to Mr. Merryweather, who was staring into his nearly empty glass, an expression of anticipation on his face.

"Another glass of wine, Merryweather?"

"What? Wine? No, I must get on. It is a goodly distance to London, and I've no wish to travel after dark. One rarely hears tales of highwaymen now, but I admit that traveling once night has fallen gives me shivers. I'm not a brave man, I fear. No, no. No more wine. Have you a message for your mother, my lord?" he asked, an avid look on his face.

"I've written her a letter, of course. If you see her you might pass on your estimate of Miss Morgan. I'm certain it will be positive, will it not? No one could meet my Phillida and not find her an absolute dear."

A startled glance was tossed her way which very nearly overset Phillida's sense of the ridiculous. It was all too obvious Mr. Merryweather couldn't believe his ears. That Lord John was besotted by his betrothed was clear—but why that should be was more than poor Mr. Merryweather could fathom. She *was* long in the tooth—which she'd admitted—and nothing like the diamonds Lord John was known to set up as his peculiars. He searched his mind for a truthful but still polite response. He didn't find it. "I will say all that is proper."

"You do that. We'll keep you no longer, Merryweather," said Lord John, leading their guest to the door. "We would not wish you to find yourself anywhere but London once dark has fallen. You've several invitations you wish to take up, do you not? Have a pleasant journey." Lucas closed the door on Merryweather on the last word and turned to lean against it. "Well?"

"Very well, Lucas. I'd no notion you were so good at my aunt's game."

Lucas strolled toward her. "Your aunt's game, m'dear?"

"Hmm-hmm."

"Would you care to explain?"

"Certainly. You manipulated that poor man finely, did you not?"

"I hope I left him convinced of the truth."

"Truth? Lucas, when you actually become as besotted of some woman as you pretended for Mr. Merry-weather's benefit, I wish to know of it."

"Then know it now," he said, an edge to his tone.

All laughter fled Phillida's face, her eyes bleak and her complexion paling in an instant. "Oh, dear. I knew it. Why, then, do you go on with this? Why did you ever begin it?"

Lord John had had no notion what to expect after blurting out such an admission. Discovering she was *distressed* was not among the reactions he'd have predicted if he'd had time to think about it. *"Now* what are you saying?"

"If there is a woman about whom you feel so deeply, why did you suggest we become betrothed—even as a ploy?"

For a moment Lord John was stunned into silence. Didn't she understand? No. Quite obviously she did not. He sighed. "Because it is clear the woman I love doesn't love me," he said through clenched teeth.

Phillida turned to hide her pain. "I'm sorry, my lord." He touched her gently. "Philly, will you trust me to know my own mind?" She nodded. "Then stop this incessant worrying. Please?" She didn't turn to him. What could he do? "Perhaps," he said, "I should explain . . ."

A tap at the door was followed by the entry of a maid bearing a tray well loaded with good things to eat. There were cold meats, a haricot made of beans and yesterday's leg of lamb, a jelly which Lucas ignored and which Phillida accepted for no other reason than that she was aware the landlady believed all women of the ton desired a sweet in their meal. There was a good country bread and butter, a dish of plum preserves made just as Lucas liked them, potatoes with a cheesy sauce that was surprisingly good—a notion Phillida told herself she'd try to reproduce—and, finally, a beef-and-kidney pie with a crust which nearly floated into the mouth all by itself.

Lord John's chance to explain was lost, and he wondered when he might again have the courage to tell Phillida it was herself he loved. Putting the problem from his mind, he concentrated on making the meal pleasant. They laughed a lot, had one or two well-battled arguments, and, in all, each enjoyed it immensely.

"The cook is very good," they told the innkeeper. He beamed at the praise to his wife. "We'll stop whenever we pass," promised Lord John as he paid the bill and added a tip for the servants. The host bowed until his nose very nearly touched his knees and personally escorted them from the inn.

Phillida didn't know whether to be glad or sorry when Lord John entered the carriage behind Flint. It was another twenty miles. Three more hours on the road during which she must hide her feelings from Lord John's perceptive eyes. Phillida searched for an innocuous topic of conversation—then told herself not to be a fool. Innocuous was *not* what was wanted. She'd ask how he felt about land enclosure, a nicely controversial subject. But, if they were in agreement on that, she'd think of something else—Napoleon's divorce of Josephine last year, citing barrenness as just cause, and marriage to Marie-Louise of Austria, perhaps.

Seven

Mrs. Morgan held one hand out to her daughter and the other to Lord John. "I am so pleased for you. I wish you both very happy indeed."

"But, Mother, didn't you understand? We left *such* a hubbub in London. Lucas insists it will soon be forgotten, but I'm embarrassed and I know you must be worried."

"My dear, if your Lucas says it'll be all right, then it is insulting to believe otherwise."

"Hear, hear! Philly, love . . ."

"Don't call me that."

". . . listen to your mother. She's a wise woman."

"Why? Because she's silly enough to allow you to do her thinking for her?" Phillida gasped. "Oh dear, I'm obviously not myself. Forgive me. Both of you."

"She's overset by it all, my lord."

Lucas nodded, his mouth primmed as when trying not to smile. "Therefore, we should forgive her, should we not?" His lips quivered, and, after a moment, he joined the woman he hoped would soon become his mother-in-law in chuckles, his eyes crinkling at the corners in that way they had.

With no thought of manipulation on his part, his natural charm made another conquest. Mrs. Morgan came very close to batting her eyelashes at him. "Very true, my lord." She laughed more freely at the storm clouds flashing in her daughter's eyes. "Phillida, you must not show your jealousy so, when another woman flirts a bit with your Lucas. He is delightful."

Phillida realized she was making a cake of herself, so she sighed overly dramatically. "I now understand my aunt's warnings. When my own mother succumbs to your wiles, I see it's true that I'll be unable to hold you, my lord. Therefore, wishing to avoid the pain of future rejection, I immediately release you from this engagement, and wish you a safe journey back to town." She held up her hand when Lucas, a frown deep on his forehead, would have spoken. "The ten-day wonder may lengthen to twelve when you, too, insert a notice that we are not to wed, but the ton is so bored it is one's duty, at least once in one's life, to give them something about which they may talk."

Phillida pretended to feel virtuous. Her mother, knowing her daughter's odd sense of humor well, laughed again. After looking from the mother to Phillida and back to Mrs. Morgan, Lord John shook his head. "I see," he said, "that I must learn when my love is hoaxing me. Phillida, I'm not wrong, am I? You aren't seriously upset with me, are you?"

She shook her head, but she'd had enough discussion of her sham engagement. It hurt too much. "Mother, is Sir Clifford at the Hall?"

Her mother blushed, a conscious look on her heart-shaped face, which, except that it lacked dimples, was very like her daughter's. She looked anywhere but at Phillida. Finally, bravely, Mrs. Morgan raised her eyes.

"Aha!" Phillida smiled broadly. "You devils you. My lord," she went on, "ours is not the only engagement for the Morgan women. When are you to announce yours, Mother?"

"Well"—Mrs. Morgan looked flustered—"now you've

returned to the country, I'm not certain just what we'll do."

Lord John and Phillida exchanged a questioning glance. "What would you have done had Phillida *not* come home just now?" he asked.

"We'd thought to make the run up to London day after tomorrow. Sir Clifford has acquired a license, and we meant to collect Phillida and go straight to a small church where a friend is the vicar. Phillida was to witness our marriage. It is our intention to stay in Clifford's town house for a few weeks' enjoyment of the Season. Besides," a lovely blush lit her cheeks, "I'm badly in need of a new wardrobe. I thought perhaps Phillida would help me choose it. You have such an eye, Lida, m'love, for material and styles."

"I should enjoy that very much."

"She may choose her trousseau at the same time," inserted Lord John, and he got a dirty look from his love. He grinned at her. "I wish her to pick light fabrics, since we'll be off to Naples."

"Italy, my lord?" asked Mrs. Morgan, her forehead suddenly corrugated with worry lines. "Isn't it dangerous, traveling so far?"

Lord John's expression darkened and his lips tightencd at the thought of the war. He gave a visible shrug, pushing the memory from his mind. "We'll travel on my yacht in a naval convoy. That way one is safe enough." It was his turn to look a trifle conscious. His cheekbones rosy, he added, "I've been asked to carry orders to our ambassador. The government is making plans, and certain conclusions are to be transmitted orally."

"When do you leave, my lord?" asked Mrs. Morgan, wondering if she'd time to arrange a suitable wedding or if her daughter's marriage must be a hole in the corner affair which would only add to the scandal surrounding the mix-up over the announcements.

"It is thought all will be in hand by the end of the summer."

Mrs. Morgan brightened. "There is time, then."

"Time, Mother?"

"To arrange your wedding, my dear, just as I've always planned. I wish it a day you will never forget."

Lucas and Phillida looked at each other. Simultaneously they shook their heads, but for very different reasons. The last thing Lucas wished was a dozen bridesmaids, a long, boring bridal breakfast at which he and Phillida must be polite to every relative each owned—including any number they wished they didn't—and every member of the ton who managed an invitation. He wanted none of that nonsense. Phillida was simply wondering how they were to stop her mother from making plans which would be difficult to cancel.

"Mother," she suggested, unable to think of another reason for changing the subject, "let's not worry about *my* wedding just now. We must plan *your* wedding instead."

"Oh no, dear. That's all settled." Mrs. Morgan frowned. "Or it was. Oh, dear. Do you think I should write Clifford?"

"I think you should invite him to dinner. Letters are rarely satisfactory, because one may not answer back directly. And now, I wish to go to my room. Lucas? May I show you yours?" She sent what could only be called a pleading look toward him. "He's to have the Green Room, is he not, Mother?"

They walked out, leaving behind Phillida's bemused mother. There was something, thought Mrs. Morgan, not quite right between those two. So obviously in love with each other! And yet, they rather warily circled, seemed not quite free to touch each other, were cautious about what was said—and apologized when unnecessary. But it was a mystery she could probe at her leisure. Now she must inform Cliffie of the complications to

their own little plot. Mrs. Morgan moved to her es-
critoire and took out paper, checked her pen before
dipping it in the ink—then let the ink dry while decid-
ing how to begin and found it necessary to dip it again.

They took two days on the road to London. Sir Clifford, after listening to Lord John and Phillida's story,
said he saw no reason to change their plans. Lord John
agreed. Since only Phillida had reservations—or more
accurately, a deep reluctance to face the ton while still
required to pretend to an engagement—it was settled.

The two men got along surprisingly well, Phillida
thought, holding the strap firmly against the motion of
the coach. Lord John and Sir Clifford rode side by side
in the morning sun and talked. In fact, she fumed, they
hadn't stopped talking from the moment they were introduced and recalled seeing each other in town. They'd
discovered several friends, two societies, and one club
in common, and the women might well have retired to
the antipodes for all the attention they received.

Phillida had always known Sir Clifford spent weeks
at a time in London, before returning, always, to her
mother's side. It had never occurred to her to wonder
what he did there. Now it seemed he attended lectures,
spent time listening to debates when Parliament was sitting, and worked on more than one committee to help
the poor.

"Mother, did you know of Sir Clifford's activities in
London?"

"What, dear? Yes, of course. We often discuss his
work—but too often he's had more than enough time to
think things through and has already had every thought
I have on a subject. Now, we may talk when he is still
excited. Dialogue is much preferable to monologues,
my dear," she said with a twinkle. "It is one reason Sir

Clifford finally found the courage to ask for my hand. He wished my company in town as well as in the country." Mrs. Morgan bit her lip. "Phillida, dear. You are truly undisturbed by my marrying another man?"

"Disturbed? You mourned my father far longer than duty demanded. Especially given his notions on the subject! He would not have wished you to spend the rest of your life in that state."

"Assuming he thought of it at all!" said Mrs. Morgan a trifle tartly, her eyes flashing in the same way Phillida's did when angry.

Phillida bit her lip. Had the perfect marriage between her parents been mussed by a wrinkle here and there?

"I'm sorry, Phillida. I shouldn't have said that, because I know how you admire your father, but he thought most social conventions silly, and mourning conventions were among those he believed particularly by the way. I never could bring myself to agree with his attitude." Mrs. Morgan patted Phillida's hand and changed the subject. "When we arrive in London, we go directly to the church. We are having such a quiet wedding, but it is my second and I didn't wish a lot of fuss. Dear Cliffie agreed. Soon we can think about *your* problems." Mrs. Morgan's forehead wrinkled—again, very like her daughter. "To begin, we must know just what the ton is saying about you and Lord John. Then we may plan countermeasures. I will write a note to Maria as soon as I have a moment."

"Maria, Mother?"

"Yes. Maria Sefton. A dear friend, Phillida. I'm certain she'll tell us all we need to know and how best to deal with it." She looked at her daughter when nothing was said. "Phillida? Dear? Are you all right?"

"You call one of the patronesses of Almack's a dear friend?"

"Yes. Certainly." Her mother looked bewildered. "Should I not? After all, it is what she is, m'love."

"I wonder you didn't tell me before my visit to Lady Brookhaven. My aunt worried, loudly and at length, about how she was to get vouchers for her countrified little niece who was so very nearly on the shelf."

"Did she? How strange. She knows Maria and I were close as inkle weavers in our youth. She might have guessed we've kept up a correspondence since I've mentioned Maria in my letters to her. I wonder why Lady Brookhaven didn't go to her for the vouchers."

Phillida looked thoughtful. "Now I think on it, I believe the Seftons only recently arrived in Town. If I hadn't tumbled into scandal's soup kettle, perhaps Lady Sefton would have come to see me." Phillida's mind continued to gnaw at her visit to her aunt, and suddenly she sat up straight. "I wonder if Lady Brookhaven would have liked that. It occurs to me to wonder if my aunt was delaying plans for Almack's until she had me safely buckled to Osbourn!"

"Are you suggesting she didn't attempt to get you vouchers?"

"I've just recalled that whenever we went anywhere where any of the patronesses happened to be, Lady Brookhaven managed to avoid all contact with each and every one. I was never once introduced to anyone who could have helped. Even at the Cowpers' breakfast! We were very late, and *there* I somehow missed being introduced to my hostess, of all things!"

"Well, at least you need not go back to your aunt. It would seem very strange if you were not to live with your mother, but, however angry you are, we mustn't cut her, my dear."

When the carriage had jounced over the last of the cobbles and finally drew up beside the unfashionable St. Mary-le-Strand neither Phillida nor her mother was much in the mood for a wedding. Lord John, leaning against one of the four pillars supporting the small portico to the church, watched the women as they brushed down each other's skirts, tut-tutted at the wrinkles, and patted their hair. He led Phillida a few paces away from her mother. "You are in a temper, m'love. Why?"

"How thoughtless men can be. My poor mother."

"I presume that makes sense?"

"Of course it does. Look at us. We are hopelessly mussed and in need of a cup of tea, and most of all, require an hour in which to primp." She stared wordlessly at Lord John, daring him to find a solution to the problem.

"One moment, lady of my heart. I'll see what I can do."

Lord John briefly consulted Sir Clifford, gesturing down the street toward a small hotel. Sir Clifford heaved a sigh, then nodded, turning to go into the church at his back, where it was his unenviable duty to talk with his friend the cleric and postpone the ceremony for an hour. Lord John approached the women. "Give me a moment and I'll arrange accommodation for you. Can you tell me which trunks or bandboxes you'll need, or should I have everything brought in? The baggage coach, thank goodness, followed us closely."

"Cliffie's valet wished to see him married. They have been together for a very long time." Mrs. Morgan drew in a deep breath. "Lord John, are you saying we may have time to change and to drink a dish of bohea and, perhaps, a few minutes' rest?"

"I'll hire you a bedroom with adjoining parlor. Then I'll send up your maids along with your boxes. Finally, I'll order you a nuncheon."

An hour later the party gathered in the church and trooped down the aisle to where the cleric awaited them. There it was discovered that Lord John had not stopped with arranging for their comfort. While the women changed he'd found a flower girl, and, when they reached the altar, he handed each woman a posy. But when he went to stand beside Sir Clifford, Phillida blinked.

"I asked him to be a witness," whispered her soon-to-be stepfather. "After all, he'll soon be family."

Phillida tried to catch Lord John's eyes but failed. It seemed he was being drawn more and more tightly into the noose. If something were not soon done, he would be trapped. It worried her so much, she had to force herself to pay attention to the simple ceremony which joined her mother and Sir Clifford.

Back in the coach for the short ride to Sir Clifford's town house, the new Lady Rogers asked her daughter about the note she'd written while sipping her tea at the hotel.

"Note?" Phillida had to think. "Oh, that. It was to a new friend, Lady Gwendolyn Troquair. I hadn't a chance before leaving town, and I wished to apprise her of what has been happening and to ask that, if she were still willing to befriend me—given the rumpus over the betrothals—she visit first thing in the morning."

Later, after a delightful if light dinner—only two courses with very few removes—prepared by Sir Clifford's French chef, Lord John took himself home. He entered the front door just as his mother came down the stairs, very obviously on her way to a party. Trailing behind her was Mr. Armitage, a kindhearted gentleman Lord John had chosen with care to hold the living at the Cambridgeshire estate's village. Lord John blinked. Kindhearted, yes, but had he the strength of character required of him, mused his lordship, wondering why the chubby vicar was in London where he had no business being.

"Well, so there you are. How like you to disappear

just when I am due to arrive," his mother broke into his thoughts. "But you deign to come home, do you? At last? Not that I blame you for playing least in sight after that hubble-bubble female played such a trick on you. Well, never mind. I took care of it. Tuttles? My cloak."

Lord John threw a startled look at Tuttles, who stared straight ahead. "What have you been *kind* enough to do, Mother?"

Lady John ignored the dangerous note in her son's voice, settling the long ends of her satin-lined pelerine more to her liking. "That ridiculous notice of engagement between you and some long-in-the-tooth, countrified hoyden, who thought to trap you, of course."

"And *how*"—Lord John frowned—"did you take care of it?"

Tuttles, fully aware of the building row, took up a position well out of the line of fire, and adopted an appropriately wooden-faced expression.

"My dear"—his mother's eyes widened in pretend innocence—"you forgot to send in a retraction before leaving town. It was very bad of you, but you mustn't worry. I did it for you the very first thing."

"You sent in a retraction." She nodded, although it wasn't a question. Lord John's temper rose astronomically—as it often did when dealing with his overly officious mother. "Without consulting me, without determining my wishes, you sent in a retraction?"

Lady John tipped her head and stared down her nose at the troublesome boy. "It was the least I could do for you. How any girl expected to get away with such a brazen plan to trap a peer into marriage I'll never know. She must be very stupid."

"You have once again jumped to conclusions. I knew I should forbid you to come to London."

"Forbid me . . . !" Her head tipped to an arrogant angle. "You can forbid me nothing. I am Lady John."

"To my sorrow I must needs acknowledge the relationship," he said more bitingly than was his wont when dealing with his mother. "It would not prevent me forbidding you house-room, however, if necessary. If you have indeed interfered in my life in such a high-handed way, then removing you from my various homes may become necessary even before I wed." He sighed. "I believed Lady Brookhaven the most thoughtless woman in Society. I commiserated with Phillida," he said in a silky tone, "on having to acknowledge such a one as a relative, but now I find I, myself, have much for which to apologize."

"Apologize? For what, pray tell?" Her pretense at bewilderment didn't ring true. "And who is Phillida?"

"My betrothed, Mother, whom, in your great wisdom, you've harmed—perhaps to the extent of destroying her reputation beyond repair. I will fall to my knees and abjectly beg her to believe I knew nothing of your designs. We'll hope she'll believe me." He sighed again. "Well, there is nothing for it. There will have to be still another announcement."

"Another? I wish I knew what you were blithering on about." But Lady John's pale complexion paled still more, revealing she understood very well.

"I will, of course, reinstate our engagement," said Lord John in an overly polite voice. "It will allow the ton another laugh at our expense, but what care you for that?"

"You'll do no such thing."

"Oh, but I *will*. I've no notion what insipid chit you've most recently chosen with the expectation I'll take her to wife as my brother meekly did the woman you chose for him. I leave it to you to tell the child of your mistake. I've chosen my own bride, Mother, and if you interfere, again, in any way, I'll"—his brow lightened with the solution which occurred to him—"I'll put you on a ship to the West Indies. You'd enjoy a long visit to your brother there, would you not?" Lady John stared at nothing. "Mother, you did hear me, did you not?"

Her eyes flew to his. "You would not put another woman before me!"

"Where do you come by such notions? We've been at daggers drawn since I went to Eton when you couldn't accept that I become independent of you in any way. I've never forgotten the friendships you spoiled, for instance. Since, it's been one dreary thing after another. It has just occurred to me that in some ways the Peninsula was more peaceful than life with you."

"If only I'd known your brother would be such a fool as to kill himself in a carriage accident!"

"Yes, you had him nicely trained from infancy, both to fear you and to obey you in all things. I thank God I escaped all that. Be warned, Mother. I will escort you aboard a ship with no qualms." He watched her for a moment before turning to the hovering vicar. "Mr. Armitage? How are you?"

"Er"—the vicar looked to Lady John for direction, but for once she paid him no heed—"I'm very well, my lord. And you?"

"As you see. I'm sorry you must, so often, witness my differences with my mother." Instinctively, Lord John attempted to ease the social strain with a change of subject. "How goes the Sunday school I asked you to establish?"

The vicar swallowed. "Sunday school, my lord?" Again his eyes flicked toward Lady John, back to her son. "Well, er—hmmm . . . Lady John . . ." Mr. Armitage looked again toward Lady John, obviously hoping for help.

It was not forthcoming.

Lord John looked to his mother. The frown he'd erased when he'd turned to make polite conversation with his vicar returned. "I see. Tutt, is Baxter available?"

"I believe your secretary is in the study, m'lord."

Lord John's brows rose. "So late? How conscientious of him. Mother, you ordered a carriage and you must not keep my horses standing. I'll wish you good night."

Lady John blinked, came out of her brown study, and nodded. She headed for the door, which Tuttles jumped to open. "Come along, Armitage."

"Do no such thing, Mr. Armitage," said Lord John.

Lord John moved into the study. After one desperate look toward Lady John, Mr. Armitage scurried after him and closed the door. Lady John started toward them, but, when the door shut practically in her face, she thought better of continuing her argument just then and left the house.

"Now, Mr. Armitage," Lord John asked, "did my mother tell you you were not to organize the Sunday school?"

"Yes, my lord." Armitage gulped. "She said teaching would only give the poor ideas above their station and that she would tell you it was a silly notion." Armitage tugged at his cravat.

"Needless to say, she told me no such thing, but simply countermanded my orders. Mr. Armitage, you do realize, do you not, that you hold your living through *my* goodwill and not *hers?*"

"Yes, my lord," gasped the vicar.

"Then you realize it is I and not my mother you must satisfy?"

"Yes, my lord." Armitage hung his head. "It is very difficult going against her. I have been guilty of cowardice, my lord."

"I'll give you another opportunity to prove yourself. Baxter will escort you to the nearest inn and hire a post chaise to return you to your vicarage." Lord John looked pensive, tossed, and caught a snuffbox. "I should like you gone before my mother returns. Will it take you long to pack?"

"No, my lord." Armitage paled. "You mean *now*, my lord?"

"Yes. Baxter will hire outriders, so you need not fear traveling at night." Lord John restrained his abominable sense of humor and refrained from adding, *Go ye and sin no more*. The vicar bowed his way from the study. "Baxter, do we have a copy of the original announcement concerning my engagement?"

"Yes, my lord."

"Good. Copy it out in your inimitably excellent hand and, once you've seen our erring vicar on his way, take the notice to the appropriate offices. Tell the editors it is to be in tomorrow's columns without fail and no retraction is to be printed—unless such is accompanied by my seal. I'll have no more interference from anyone. Bringing Miss Morgan around to a proper frame of mind is problem enough without additional and extraneous difficulties caused by the pair of besoms to whom we are related."

With difficulty Baxter kept a straight face. "Yes, my lord. Is there anything else I can do for you this evening?"

"No. Once you've dropped off those notices, you may have whatever may be left of it for yourself. Oh, for Armitage's expenses, there is a pouch in the top drawer of my desk. It should be sufficient."

"Yes, my lord." The secretary began gathering up his things.

"Baxter," said his lordship, still pensive.

"Yes, my lord?"

"Have you ever been in love, Baxter?"

Baxter blinked. "No, my lord."

"Too bad, Baxter. I am much in need of advice."

The secretary folded his hands. "Perhaps I might help in some way?"

"They say true love never runs smoothly. I wish I could get it running any way at all. I'd smooth it out later."

"I don't believe I understand, my lord."

"It is simple enough, Baxter. I have found the love of my life. Would you believe she is the first woman I've known since I was breeched—other than my mother— that I can't wind around my fingers and induce to love me?"

Baxter smiled. "I don't believe it, my lord." When Lucas glanced at him, he continued. "Perhaps the lady is shy, hiding her feelings from you?"

"Shy? Phillida?" Lucas shook her head. "My love hasn't a shy bone in her body. You'll have to think up another way to encourage me."

"Yes, my lord. I'll put my mind to it."

Lord John assumed Baxter was joshing him, but he wasn't. Baxter, like all Lord John's dependents, would go to the ends of the earth for him.

The knocker banged on Sir Clifford's front door. Phillida, at the top of the stairs to the entrance hall, heard a low-voiced argument between Rutgers, Sir Clifford's butler, and whomever had arrived at such an odd hour. Their voices floated up to her as she descended, and she recognized Lady Gwendolyn's. Surprised, she moved more quickly, fearing Sir Clifford's toffee-nosed butler would shut the door in her friend's face.

"Gwendolyn," said Phillida, "do come in. How nice of you to welcome me back to London so quickly. Rutgers, take Lady Gwendolyn's things and I will, myself, escort her to . . ." Phillida chuckled. "Oh. Gwen, dear, I have, myself only just stepped foot in this house. I don't know where to go so we may be private."

She looked at Rutgers for guidance, but he raised his nose another notch. Sir Clifford's new stepdaughter was obviously the hoyden rumor made her out to be.

Phillida frowned. When necessary she could play the great lady, and now, perceiving the direction of the butler's thoughts, she did so. She and Gwendolyn were soon ensconced in a small back parlor with orders they were not to be bothered until she rang.

"Now, Gwen, tell me what is being said."

"The mix-up is talked of everywhere, Phillida. Lady Brookhaven loudly proclaims her innocence, that she had no idea Lord John was courting you. No one believes her. Lady John is calling you names, but no one ever listens to her, I'm told. The fact you disappeared also has tongues wagging. It is widely believed you did so to escape the talk. No one mentioned that Lord John also disappeared—until the second retraction appeared."

Phillida straightened. "Second retraction?"

Gwendolyn grimaced. "I feared you might not have heard." She pulled a folded newspaper from her oversize reticule. "This came out the day following Brookhaven's denial there had ever been any understanding between you and himself."

Phillida skimmed the notice, which denied her betrothal to Lord John. For just a moment she wondered if he had inserted it without word to her, and then she told herself not to be a widgeon. Lord John had promised to do nothing without prior agreement, and he wasn't a man who lightly gave his word. "Who could have inserted it? How could this have happened?"

"Because of it, the ton is quite willing to believe the worst of you, despite Mr. Merryweather's word you and Lord John were visiting your mother. It seems he saw you and Lord John traveling together. Later, after the second retraction, he let it slip you were *without a chaperon*. He insisted, however, that Lord John clearly stated you were engaged."

"Lord John suggested we use Mr. Merryweather's well-known weakness for gossip to our advantage."

"He was made to suffer agonies once this notice appeared. He says, but weakly, it must be in error." Gwendolyn tapped the paper Phillida clutched. "Phillida, dear, what does it mean?"

"This notice? I wish I knew."

"You don't think Lord John had it inserted in your absence for some reason of his own?" asked Gwendolyn hesitantly.

"Is *that* the ton's conclusion?"

"It's only one story. It was inserted, one is also told, because you are a hoyden who attempted to trap a peer, any peer, into marrying you. It is said by some that you yourself placed the first two announcements."

"I am said to have engaged myself without their knowledge to two men at the same time? I am believed to be so stupid? Oh no. Not *stupid*," said Phillida, her tone acid. "The gabble-grinders wish to know how soon I'll find myself ensconced in Bedlam, do they not?"

Gwendolyn laughed. "Thank goodness you've not lost your sense of the ridiculous."

Phillida, not at all certain she was jesting, let that pass. But now the notice had appeared—no matter what hand had inserted it—perhaps it was for the best. She could efface herself the rest of this Season, making herself useful on some of the charitable committees her mother expected to join, and then, next Season, when all the fuss had died down to mere murmurs, perhaps she might attend a soiree or two. She sighed.

"Phillida? Are you very upset?"

"Upset? Why should I be upset? I am a born clown, a

regular Grimaldi, didn't you know? In an earlier age I'd have been the king's jester with bells on my cap." She grimaced. "Oh, it is such a hobble, is it not? I can't think where it will end."

"I'm sorry. I came at once because I felt I must warn you before you went, innocently, into the tumult which will greet your first appearance and, of course, I didn't know when that would be."

Phillida blenched at the notion of facing the ton with no warning. "Lucas!" Color raced to fill her pale cheeks. "What if *he* goes out . . . ? Oh, dear. I hope I'm not too late." She rang the bell and tapped a toe until Rutgers, in his dilatory way, came to discover her wishes. She frowned at him. "Rutgers, where may I find Sir Clifford?"

"If Sir Clifford wished you to know his whereabouts, I'm sure he'd have informed you," responded the butler impertinently. He actually smirked at having an opportunity to put this upstart into her place.

"Hmm," said the upstart thoughtfully. "I wonder if Lady Rogers really wishes a butler who doesn't understand her little ways. Perhaps I should have a talk with my mother about *changes*. Having a mistress in the house makes a difference, does it not? A woman will not allow things to go on in the rough and ready way of a bachelor establishment, will she?"

Rutgers paled. He was not a particularly intelligent man, and it hadn't occurred to him the new mistress might wish to Make Changes. His nose dropped a fraction. "Sir Clifford is in the salon awaiting the new Lady Rogers, Miss Morgan," he said, suddenly obsequious.

"Very good. You said that very nicely. And it really wasn't all that difficult, was it?"

Rutgers blinked. "Is that all, Miss Morgan?"

Phillida sighed. It really was beneath her to bait such easy prey as Rutgers. "Yes, thank you. You may go." He left, and Phillida turned to Gwen. "Do come and meet my stepfather. I must ask a favor of him—immediately—or I wouldn't be so rag-mannered as to drag you into company when you didn't come prepared for it."

Gwendolyn shook her head. "Mr. Diggory awaits me." She blushed rosily. "We were about to leave for a musical evening when I received your note."

Mr. Diggory? thought Phillida but put the thought aside until she had more time to consider the possibilities. "I am so glad you came."

Phillida again rang for the butler, and, when Rutgers appeared, obviously put out at being called again so soon, she went with them to the door, where she waved her friend good-bye. Then she hurried up to the salon. She entered, not at all embarrassed to find her mother in Sir Clifford's arms. "I'd apologize, except I think I'll find you in the same situation often and apologies would become a dead bore. I'd leave you in peace, but I fear something terrible has happened and word must be sent to Lord John at once—hopefully before he goes to his club or wherever he may be off to."

"My dear, you are making no sense."

"I don't suppose I am." Phillida drew in a deep breath and calmly relayed Lady Gwendolyn's news. "So you see," she finished, "Lord John may find himself the center of a new storm. In which case, who knows what he'll say or do?" She realized she still held the paper, and handed it over.

"Oh, dear."

"What an inadequate expression of your feelings, Mother."

"But, my dear, I *can't* say what I was thinking. That would be totally unacceptable. Is there no end to this nonsense?"

"I wonder who inserted this latest notice," said Sir

Clifford, reading where Phillida pointed. "It is rather crudely worded, wouldn't you agree?"

Phillida sighed. "*Nastily*, you mean. It was meant to hurt me, I think."

"Yes. I think that too. I won't wait to have a carriage harnessed. Rutgers must find me a hackney. With any luck I'll catch Lord John before he goes out. He won't be happy about this, but his temper will be still more exasperated if he discovers it by chance from a friend—or, worse yet, from an enemy!"

Sir Clifford left on the words.

Eight

Flint entered the Running Footman and hurried to the corner where her father sat with another retired butler, their eyes glued to the board game between them. "Good evening, Mr. Druggles, Father," she said in greeting.

"Ahh, you're home. That was a quick trip."

"As you know," said Flint not only mendaciously, but in a tone meant to be overheard, "we went to apprise our mother of our engagement. Our mother had a nice surprise for us. She, too, was engaged and planned an immediate wedding here in London. Thus our return. She is become Lady Rogers, and we are now established in Sir Clifford's town house."

Mr. Porterman glanced around. The groups seated around tables and on benches against the walls had overheard, and a buzz of conversation rose around the room. He nodded to his friend, who obligingly picked up the game board and, with a muttered word in Flint's general direction, took himself off. Flint sat.

"Now," said Porterman, leaning forward and putting his head close to his daughter's, "lower your voice to a mere roar, and tell me what in blazes is going on. Is your miss engaged to Lord John or is she not?" He waited, very obviously curious for her answer.

"I was hoping *you* had news for *me*. The latest notice appeared while we were gone." Bitterness crept into her voice as she continued. "Sir Clifford's servants weren't behindhand in telling me what is thought of my much-maligned miss. Worse, they treat her with as little respect as they dare. It isn't to be tolerated. I don't suppose you know who's responsible? My only thought is that Lady Brookhaven has flipped her wig entirely—she still wears one, you know."

"It's said she chortled herself into a spasm when she saw the second retraction. That bit of gossip was going the rounds late the morning it appeared, which was—my goodness—only yesterday! Her glee indicates, I think, she hadn't a notion about it beforehand, but was pleased to see it. She denies having inserted it."

"Then who . . . Ah. Mr. Tuttles. I hoped you'd come by."

"Shouldn't be here at all, so we'd best hurry. It doesn't set a good example to the younger servants when the butler slips out, but I thought you might want what news I have."

"You're looking rather grim."

"You would, too, if you'd been in my shoes this past hour. Thank you kindly, luv," he said to the barmaid who followed him to the fireplace and handed him a heavy-wet. "What a set-to," he continued once the wench was gone. "I suppose I should be used to it by now." He drank. "I need this badly. A ball of fire might be more welcome still—but no," he decided, sadly. "We need our wits about us, so I'll abstain from gin." He drank deeply of the ale, however, very nearly finishing it.

"Mr. Tuttles, you speak in riddles," scolded Flint.

"I suppose I do. I don't know if I'm on my head or my heels. That last notice? *Lady John* inserted it in Lord John's name."

"Life amongst the nobs do get complicated, don't it?" asked Porterman, manfully holding back his chuckles. "*Now* what will happen, do you suppose?"

"Lord John has ordered the engagement notice re-inserted. Mr. Baxter is taking care of that tonight, so it will run tomorrow."

"Won't the breakfast tables be jumping wild?"

"Father, hold your tongue, do. My miss is distraught and unhappy."

"It is good news for our plans, is it not, that she's unhappy?" suggested Tuttles a trifle diffidently.

"How dare you say such a thing?"

"She wouldn't be unhappy if she cared not a rap for his lordship, now would she? We do want them to love each other, don't we?"

Flint thought about that and a small smile grew into a grin. "I see. Very astute, Mr. Tuttles. And his lordship's feelings?"

"He was *very* angry with his mother. He was threatening her with Dire Consequences if she dared interfere with his life ever again."

"But," objected Flint, "couldn't that have been anger at her interference and nothing to do with Miss Morgan?"

"He's been angry with his mother before—but never like this." Tuttles frowned. "Why do you doubt his feelings? After all, they're engaged, and I don't believe Lord John would ask a woman to marry him if he weren't partial to her. It's my belief he loves her very much, despite his express desire I find him a docile, not to say complaisant, wife, which you must admit Miss Morgan is *not.*"

Flint frowned. "Miss Morgan mutters. I can't help but overhear." She eyed the two men. If they were to help, they must know the truth, so she must break what she considered a sacred confidence—given she'd heard what wasn't meant for her ears. Still, she needed help, so . . . She plunged in. "Mr. Tuttles, can you think of a reason why those two might have entered into an engagement for show—not meant to go so far as the altar, I mean?"

"What are you suggesting?" he asked sharply.

"That, despite Lord John's anger, the engagement is not real. That, for reasons known only to themselves, they are hoaxing the ton. That, in fact, the engagement doesn't mean they fell in love—as we wish them to do. Far worse, they intend, eventually, to break it off." Flint drew in a deep breath and frowned. "You see, Miss Morgan's reason for finding a husband is gone: her mother planned her marriage before hearing of her daughter's engagement. Miss Morgan's spinsterhood was obviously never the deterrent to her mother's happiness she was made to believe it might be."

"I don't know what to say. I'd have sworn—Lady John has been told in no uncertain terms she's never to interfere in his lordship's life, and that *might* be all . . ." Tuttles rubbed his chin. "Old friend," he asked, turning to Porterman, "have you any words of wisdom?"

"Sham engagements are dangerous things. They just might find themselves leg-shackled in spite of contrary plans."

"My lady would not like that. She has the wisdom to fear Lord John would feel himself trapped, fear he'd become bitter, that he'd hate her for it."

"My gentleman would never be so low as to blame the lady for what was his own fault. I'm certain as can be the idea of an engagement must have come from him, you see."

"But she agreed. She'll see herself as responsible."

"Will you two cease argufying about which of your fools will act the more noble? The important thing is to discover how to bring them to their senses and make them admit they love each other." Porterman leaned back and looked from one to the other.

"But *do* they?" asked Flint and Tuttles together.

"'Course they do. But each believes the other doesn't."

Silence followed Porterman's analysis, and then Flint suggested, "If it is true they love each other, but the engagement is, nevertheless, a hoax, our job is more difficult than ever, is it not?"

"How so, Missus Flint?"

"Why, 'tis obvious. Neither will allow the other to see their real feelings. Each will assume the other happy with the hoax—at least, so long as no one is trapped—and both will do their best to live by the arrangement."

Tuttles sighed. "Your daughter inherited your bone-box, old friend. No feathers under that pretty bonnet of hers."

"I'll assume you believe that to be a compliment," said Flint a trifle chillingly, "but it doesn't further our discussion. What is to be done?"

"First off, we must scotch the rumors about Miss Morgan. She is not a brass-faced hussy—among the politer names she's being called—who would do what's being said she did," said her father.

Flint nodded. "I agree. Once she thinks a bit, the poor dear will be afraid to put her nose out of doors. She's already suggested she live retired this Season and work with her mother on whatever committees Lady Rogers joins. But I don't think the notion appeals. So, yes. Those rumors must be contradicted."

"Miss Morgan's feelings are important, of course, but it is far more important," said Tuttles, very much on his dignity, "that they be contradicted so that Lord John won't be embarrassed to be seen with her."

"You have, as usual, the wrong cat by the tail," sniffed Flint.

"Now, now, none of that," said Porterman. "For both their sakes, the rumors must be made harmless by starting up contrary notions. 'Tis easy enough for me to slip the word into conversations, but I must know what to say."

The butler and abigail ceased glowering at each other and the trio got back to work.

Mr. Porterman suggested, "First off, we must assure everyone that Miss Morgan had nothing to do with any of the notices."

"Yes," agreed Flint. "Do you think we might distort the reason she and Lord John left London? If they were called home by her mother because Mrs. Morgan wished help preparing for her wedding, would that help? I think Mrs. Morgan—I mean Lady Rogers— would understand it was for her daughter and would not contradict such a rumor."

"Then we may take it she won't interfere. It is near the truth and will be believed. With that reason for leaving, no one will think a thing—well, not so *much*—of Lord John and Miss Morgan traveling away from London just when the two notices were discovered by half the ton and word passed to the other half before the cat could lick its nose."

"That might work," said Porterman. "Could I perhaps let it be known Lord Brookhaven inserted his retraction with no encouragement from anyone?"

"No, don't do that," said Flint. "I don't think we should stretch the truth more than necessary. . . ."

"I agree," said Tuttles. "Besides, we can't lay it at Lord Brookhaven's feet, because it is known Lord John introduced his lordship to a fellow member of one of his societies the very day Lord John and Miss Morgan left town. Whether or not Lord John also helped Lord Brookhaven with the first notice of retraction isn't of concern." Tuttles drew in a deep breath. "What *is* necessary is to make it clear *Lady John* inserted the fourth notice and that it was *not* with Lord John's authority."

"I dislike deliberately hurting anyone," said Flint,

"but Lord John's mother must be sacrificed. There is no way to wrap it up in clean linen. It must get about that she interfered and, still more important, acted without Lord John's knowledge and certainly without his approval."

"So I'm to knit two things into my gossip," said Porterman. "The first is that Miss Morgan had nothing to do with any notice, and the second that Lady John tried, once again, to run, if not ruin, her son's life."

"That's it." Tuttles relaxed, finished his brew with a last long swig.

Flint sighed, yawned, then stretched, her hands pressed to the back of her waist. "Father, I'm getting old. I didn't used to be worn to a thread by a few hours' travel, but I tell you I'm looking forward to my bed tonight. I'd best get back to Sir Clifford's, because my miss may wish an early night as well—oh, I do hope so!" She yawned again. "Another time we'll deal with the problem of making our young people admit they love each other."

The morning sun streamed in the tall front windows. "I'm not going and that's that." Phillida backed away from Lord John. She glanced toward her mother, whose concentration was fully on her tatting in the bright morning light. Phillida knew that was nonsense: her mother could tat in her sleep. On the other hand, the older woman had settled herself at the far end of the drawing room and perhaps she *wasn't* listening.

"The morning is lovely," said Lord John in a coaxing voice. "The sun is shining. The weather is perfect. My horses need exercise. I wish a pretty lady by my side. Come, love," said his lordship. "You mustn't disappoint all the gossips when they so wish to see us together.

Why, what would they have to talk about if we don't go for our usual drive?"

"Probably the fact we *didn't*." She shook her head. "Please. It's over now. And better that way."

Lord John frowned. "Over?"

"Two engagements. Two retractions. It's over."

"Nonsense. I've explained what my mother did."

"I appreciate that you came to tell me personally. Sir Clifford told me about it when he came home last night, so you needn't have done so, but it was kind of you to . . ." She stared. "Lord John?" She blinked as the sound she'd heard was repeated. "Are you *growling?*"

"Phillida, you must have only half the story, although I can't for the life of me understand why Sir Clifford didn't tell you the whole. Worse, you didn't read this morning's papers, did you?" he asked.

"Why, no. I . . ." She couldn't very well explain that, depressed by the future loss of his company, she'd not been in the mood to do so.

Lord John turned and raised his voice to ask, "And you, Lady Rogers? Did you read them?"

"Read what? The papers? I never do so. I'm a letter writer, Lord John. I prefer to receive news directly from my friends."

"And last night. Sir Clifford didn't tell you what I'd done?"

Phillida glanced at her mother, who had returned to her tatting. She turned back to Lord John. "Lucas, Mother went up to bed when Sir Clifford went off to warn you of what had happened. I went up directly after Sir Clifford told me Lady John inserted the retraction. He called after me to wait, but I was . . . tired. From our trip to town, you know. I'd stayed up too long as it was, waiting for him."

"And this morning he didn't tell you?"

"He was gone. Lord John—Lucas," she corrected herself at his quick scowl, "what *have* you done?"

"We are still officially engaged, Philly, my dear. . . ."

"Don't call me that."

"Or should one say re-engaged? I'm not quite certain exactly how to state it—given the circumstances."

"I know we didn't agree to break it off, but . . ."

"No buts. The newest notice appeared this morning."

Phillida slumped against the wall. "You . . . ?"

"I sent it in last night."

"And you're suggesting we go for a drive in the Park? Today?"

"I'm suggesting we behave just as usual."

She shook her head. "I can't do it."

"Phillida, my dear," he said softly, "believe me when I say that you must. Lady Rogers," he said, raising his voice, "tell Phillida that it would be best to behave as if nothing had happened."

Phillida looked at her mother.

"My dear, if that look is a question asking my opinion, I agree with Lord John. If you laugh off that last retraction, pretend it is a great joke, then everyone will forget it quickly enough. If you creep around as if you were guilty of some crime, then that's the way you'll be judged. Run along and get your parasol, Phillida. You mustn't forget your tendency to freckle. Given how hard we worked all winter to fade the last of them, I think you'd be very careful not to add new ones to your complexion."

"Freckles?" Phillida looked bewildered. "Mother, you are worried about *freckles* when we are in the midst of the biggest farce the ton has ever seen?"

"My dear, the time to worry about freckles is *before* they appear. The farce, as you call it, will go away with far less effort than it would take to clear your complexion again."

"Lucas!" said Phillida, her expression stormy. "If you *dare* to laugh . . ."

"Listen to your mother, love. She has her priorities in the proper order—not that I wouldn't find it great sport," he added, with a quirk to his brows, "to count each and every freckle that dares make an appearance across your delightful little nose."

Phillida blushed, glared, and left. When Lucas turned on such charm she found she was as weak as any other woman he honored with such teasing.

"Is she very upset?" he asked once the door closed behind her.

"Very."

"What can I do, Lady Rogers?"

"Exactly what you are doing. Take her out where the two of you can be seen to be on good terms. Laugh at innuendoes concerning the various announcements. Unfortunately, no one will have the courage to ask about them outright—which would make things far easier, would it not? Contradicting rumors is so difficult. One must *live* the truth and *show* that there is nothing in the talk going around. I dislike most," added Lady Rogers, "the fact Phillida is being called such names."

"I haven't heard. Tell me."

"Well, I don't know the whole of it, I fear, but my maid was very grim this morning and I got out of her that Phillida is thought a hoyden and, at best, rather stupid—to have inserted those original notices, you know?"

"I can guess at the rest. Brass-faced and hussy would be the least of it. Tuttles will know." Lady Rogers looked confused. Lord John grinned. "My butler. Wellington could use him in his intelligence organization. Don't worry. Tuttles is on my side, and since I'm betrothed to her, he'll uphold Phillida's honor as well." He looked up as Phillida returned to the salon. She was a picture in a bonnet he'd not yet seen and a dress he particularly liked. "You'll do," he said when he'd caught his breath. "Yes, my love, you'll do very well indeed." Why, he wondered, had he ever thought her plain?

Lord John stopped again and again to say a few words to friends and acquaintances as he tooled his team through the Park. Finally he noticed Mr. Merryweather strolling toward them and nudged Phillida. "Our friend with the big mouth, love. We must speak to *him* if we speak to no others, and I tell you frankly, I'm very tired of speaking to anyone but you. Ah, Merryweather, good day to you," he said as their quarry stopped beside the carriage. "I see you reached town safely."

"Aye. So I did." Merryweather looked from one to the other, obviously irritated. He then proceeded to disprove Lady Rogers's belief that no one would speak to the point. "I don't suppose you would tell me if there is to be still another notice in tomorrow's editions? You know how I like to be first with the news. It would be a kindness in you to give me a hint," he said wistfully, "especially since I suffered so from what you told me before."

"I'm sure you did your best under the circumstances," said Phillida. Her eyes narrowed as she remembered one tidbit from Lady Gwendolyn's news. "Tell me, did you mention that I was traveling without chaperon before or after the notice retracting our engagement appeared?"

Merryweather puffed out his reddening cheeks. "*After,* Miss Morgan. I attempted to make sense of what I'd seen and been told. If you were *not* engaged, you should not have been traveling under Lord John's protection. I asked his mother about it. She explained . . ." He broke off when he noticed Lord John's expression harden. "Well, what should I have done?"

"I think you might have accepted," said Lucas

smoothly, "that we were indeed on the road to Miss Morgan's mother—that it was a three-stage journey and that, since we're engaged, we'd done nothing wrong in being together when the trip did not involve spending a night along the way. Besides that, surely you know my mother after so many years' acquaintance?"

"Don't be too angry with him, Lucas," said Phillida, patting his tense arm. "Very obviously the poor man is easily led. Your mother holds strong opinions, does she not, and I'm certain she allowed him benefit of them, did she not?" she asked, turning back to look at her nemesis.

Merryweather didn't know whether to be angry at Miss Morgan's insult or to accept the excuse she'd given him. One glance at Lord John's angry features and he settled for the excuse. "Lady John, as you say, was vocal in her assurances you could not possibly be engaged to Miss Morgan. In fact, she had in tow a young lady she hinted, broadly, was to be the next Lady John."

"Did she indeed? *Another* one? Poor mother. She'll not give up thrusting those limp little misses at me until I've tied myself safely to my own true love."

Merryweather put his mind to worrying over Lord John's wry comment. He brightened. "I remember. Last autumn it was a Miss Townsend, was it not? And during the Season when you were on leave," he added, getting into the swing, "I believe there was a Lady Maria and before that—"

"Too bad you didn't remember all that much sooner," interrupted Lord John. "My mother has long attempted to interest me in women of *her* choice. I don't know if you noticed, Merryweather, but not a single one of them was just in my style."

Merryweather looked much struck by that thought. "Nor, I must say, was this latest young lady. Rather dull-looking, very quiet. I'd say she lived in a dreamworld all her own." Merryweather thought about the high fliers Lord John had had in keeping. He grinned. "No, not in your style, my lord." Then he looked at Miss Morgan. It occurred to him that Miss Morgan wasn't exactly in the proper style either, and he opened his mouth to say so. Before he could speak his gaze met Lord John's and he closed his mouth with a snap.

"Just so," said Lord John dryly. "I'd forget that last thought if I were you, because," he added softly, "it simply isn't true. Miss Morgan is very much in my style, whatever a casual glance might suggest. She is merely more subtle and much less obvious about it."

"I see." Merryweather blinked. "I *think* I see." He blinked again and shook his head as a vision of a long-legged sleepy-eyed blonde entered his mind. Lord John's mistresses *had* all been alike. "No, I don't," he finished with a confused look.

Lord John grinned. "Just accept the fact I've found the one woman who can knock my equilibrium to flinders and who, in her inimitable way, will, if I know her, keep me off center for the rest of our lives." He looked down and met Phillida's bemused look. He smiled, his eyes warming in *such* a way.

Phillida blushed rosily and turned to look straight ahead. She *must* remember he was merely acting as he was expected to act, was pretending to feel for her those emotions proper to their making a love match. In fact, she should remember that she, too, was expected to play a part. She turned back to him, allowed her face to show her real feelings, and watched the appearance of an arrested expression, something she'd have interpreted as hope under other situations—and then it disappeared to be replaced, just before he turned away, with a rather bleak look.

Phillida wished Merryweather would disappear in a puff of wizard's smoke. Just possibly she'd find the courage to probe delicately into feelings she couldn't quite believe she'd seen. Not that he could have really wished her to love him, could he? After all, that wasn't part of their agreement. No, she must have misinterpreted what she thought she'd seen. Most likely he'd been thinking of something entirely different.

Lord John excused them and kept the pace to a strict trot, concentrating on holding the young team together and using that as an excuse not to talk. He was afraid that if he allowed himself to speak, he'd ask what she really felt for him, whether there was truth behind that look he'd seen—but the fear that she was merely an excellent actress and living up to their agreement to fool the ton was too strong. He didn't want to be in public when he was told she didn't love him and couldn't see herself ever loving him and what's more had never given him the slightest indication she did or could. The pain would be too much to hide.

"Sir Romney, why are you in town so soon after your dear wife's death?" said Lady John, grasping the baronet's sleeve tightly.

"It has been well over a year, Lady John," said Sir Romney warily.

"Has it?" Lady John looked at the young miss trailing along behind her, the chit's mind obviously elsewhere. She sighed. Such a good choice for her son. The girl would never interfere with Lady John's running of things, which was just what was wanted if only her benighted son could be brought to see it. But Sir Romney . . . "Well, if it has been so long, it is time for you to be looking about you for another wife, is it not?" She drew the young woman forward and gritted her teeth when the girl seemed to wake from a dream at the pressure on her arm. "Now here is a delightful child. Just the sort . . . Sir Romney, where do you think you are going?"

He turned back, his face grim. "I've discovered I must return home at once." He avoided the eyes of the young woman whom he'd not yet met and, if he could avoid it, would not. "I must think over some old gossip I thought should be dismissed from mind—that it was too late for me—but seeing you, Lady John, has made me reconsider. Good day," he added, making the polite words sound something less than polite. He bowed, turned on his heel, and stalked off.

Lady John stared after him, wondering what the poor man could possibly be talking about. Demented with grief, she decided, unaware she'd once interfered in a love match.

"Don't know if you're interested," said Mr. Porterman to his daughter, "but I believe we may have given Sir Romney the office to move into action."

"Oh?" asked Flint, daintily sipping from her half-pint of ale. Her mind hadn't been occupied by the baronet's problems, but she was curious.

"Yes. His valet was in this morning. Seems he spent half the night packing. Mind, they aren't going directly to Tunbridge Wells to propose to his old love, but Sir Romney muttered about going there soon. Maybe."

"You wily old gaffer," said Flint admiringly.

"I don't know as how it was me," responded her father. "Seems Sir Romney ran into Lady John last night and came home ranting and raving he wouldn't let her do it to him again."

Tuttles approached, and they regaled him with the story. "Lady John is blind as a bat when it comes to seeing anything beyond her own wishes." He shook his head. "Someone needs to convince her otherwise. Now, about our plot, where we, of course, do know best—what's to do?"

Flint said. "The question my lady wants answered is *why* Lord John reinstated the engagement."

"Good question," said Porterman. "Seems if it was a mock engagement they'd entered into for reasons we don't know, then that would have been a good way of getting out of it." Porterman looked from one to the other.

Flint bridled. "Not good at all. It would have hurt my lady."

"Lord John wouldn't do that for the world, but . . ." Tuttles looked solemnly from one to the other and, leaning until the three heads nearly touched, said, "Whatever the original reason for their ploy, he *has* fallen in love with Miss Morgan, but doesn't know how to turn their sham engagement into a real one, so is holding things as they are in the hopes all will come right in the end." He sighed. "What I don't see is, if they both love the other, what is stopping them?"

"If it is, as we believe, a sham, then they *must* have agreed on a way to end it. And if it is to end, neither would wish to let the other know the ending would hurt—believing, you see, the other still wishes the end to come so of course one can't tell the other about changing their minds or about falling in love. . . ." Flint looked from one bemused man to the other. "Why do you look like that?"

"I don't know about Tuttles, daughter, but I'm confused."

"I didn't quite follow the words, but I got the sense," said Tuttles soothingly when Flint began to bristle. "Neither will let the other know how they feel now, thinking the other still feels the way they did at first."

"See, daughter? A nice choice of words makes a thing perfectly clear."

"I don't see any difference." Flint pouted, then realized how silly that was. "Anyway, if we assume that is true, what can we do?"

"Tell each what the other is thinking?" suggested Porterman.

"Can't do *that!*" said Flint and Tuttles in unison.

"Why not? Seems the simplest way."

Tuttles looked at Flint. Flint waved her hand. "You say it, since you have such a way with words," she suggested, ending with a grin which told Tuttles she wasn't holding a grudge.

"It's simple enough. If we do any such a thing, the fact we'd been gossiping becomes obvious, which fact we daren't reveal." Tuttles noted Flint's agreement. "So we wait. I don't see we can do anything else."

"Perhaps," said Flint slowly, "if all else fails, we will *have* to open our budget to one or the other or to both—*whatever* propriety suggests to the contrary."

Wearing long faces, they stared at each other, worrying at the mere possibility of having to violate a basic unwritten rule of service: one simply didn't allow one's master or mistress to know one gossiped about them.

Nine

Sir Clifford accepted the coffee his lady poured for him. He sipped and sighed—a contented and very happy sigh. Then it occurred to him Phillida was not her usual cheerful self. He sipped again, this time without tasting the pleasant brew, and sighed a second time, rather morosely.

"You're looking excessively pensive, Cliffie. What can I do?"

"I'm not certain, m'dear." He debated whether to put his oar into what might be very deep waters. It then occurred to him that his marriage had made him a father. Fathers were required to help unhappy daughters. Reaching that conclusion, he asked, "Have you noticed that Phillida is not as buoyant as one expects her to be?"

"Yes."

Sir Clifford's brows arched. "Is that terse answer by way of warning me off, m'love?"

It was Lady Rogers's turn to heave a great sigh. She set down her cup and folded her hands. "It is nothing more than agreement. I *wish* I knew what Aunt Emily did to subdue her lively nature so thoroughly."

"You blame your aunt? That's a possibility, I suppose."

"I've thought and thought and can come up with nothing but that Lady Brookhaven convinced Phillida she must suppress her . . . her . . . well, one could call it *roguishness*, I suppose, in order to win her man. "Now, having done so, Phillida daren't allow herself free rein for fear she'll lose him."

Sir Clifford considered his wife's analysis carefully before dismissing it. "M'dear, do you really think Phillida such a weak Nellie she'd allow anyone to put a bridle on her tongue?"

"You don't know my aunt."

"True. But I know our Lida. She might pretend in front of her hostess in order to avoid confrontation—although I find even that a bit much to believe—but, say she did so much, she'd not allow another to be fooled. Particularly not the man she loves. She'd think it dishonorable."

"I see *exactly* what you mean." The new Lady Rogers mused a bit more, but still found no other answer. "Then what is the problem?"

"Wouldn't you say she was distracted, on the verge of anger, perhaps"—Sir Clifford watched his wife closely—"rather than upset when she came to ask me to warn Lord John . . ." He trailed off.

Lady Rogers frowned. "I couldn't quite put my finger on it, but, yes, one could say her feathers were excessively ruffled."

He was pleased his judgment hadn't been at fault. "I've a notion which I think exceedingly strange, but for what it's worth, here it is. Emma, you don't think she suspected Lord John of inserting the notice himself—and was sending warning *just in case* he hadn't?"

Lady Rogers blinked. "Surely not." She stared. "But she *said* . . . at least, she suggested . . . but then . . ."

"Careful, love. You are dithering."

Lady Rogers bit her lip. "I distinctly heard her say he shouldn't have reinstated the engagement by putting in still *another* notice."

"When was this?"

"Yesterday when he came to take her driving. She said it was for the best that it was over." Sir Clifford's brows rose in query. The little lines marring Lady Rogers's forehead deepened. "Cliffie, you don't suppose, do you, there is something, hmm, a trifle *fishy* about their engagement?"

"It begins to smell that way," he said with a grin, but immediately sobering. "Assuming they'd agreed to play a havey-cavey game for reasons I don't pretend to understand, why would Phillida be unhappy?"

"Because Phillida is so much in love with Lord John she can't see straight?" suggested Lady Rogers promptly. "At least, I think she is. No," she contradicted herself, "I know she is. If it *is* a plot and *he* doesn't love *her,* then, of course, she'd be unhappy."

"But he does. I'm very nearly certain he does. At least, the way he looks at her and occasionally touches her—yes, I think he loves her. . . . But then again, they don't quite have that freedom toward each other one expects when . . . But they wouldn't, would they, if . . . Oh, I don't know."

"Now who is dithering?" Lady Rogers rose and placed a hand on her new husband's shoulder. "Could we ask them to clarify the situation?"

"Ask Lord John if the two of them set out to make may-game of the ton, but have now, independently, fallen in love and each wishes to make it a real engagement, but is afraid the other does not?" Sir Clifford's mind boggled at such a conversation. He shook his head. "I couldn't," he said, softening the faint reprimand by placing his hand over hers. "Would you, instead, care to probe your daughter's feelings? Not about the plot, if there is one. One can't suggest that sort of flummery unless *they* do."

"I always know how Phillida feels." Contradicting herself, Lady Rogers added, "Then again, she'd never let me know if she thought I'd worry." She sighed hugely. "Sometimes you'd think *she's* the mother and I the daughter, the way she treats me."

Sir Clifford chuckled. "It is a fault in her father. He raised her to be responsible for those around her, but no longer you, m'love. You are *my* delightful responsibility and it is my agreeable duty to care for you, and so I shall tell her the next time she impinges on my prerogative. I wonder why she thinks you cannot care for yourself?" he finished on a laughing note.

Lady Rogers chuckled obediently as she was meant to do, but was soon serious again. "Since her father thought me incompetent, Phillida does too. In the most loving and kindhearted way, of course. It's embarrassing."

"I will," said Sir Clifford, keeping his features perfectly sober, "inform her you have grown up and are capable of blowing your own nose now."

"You do that." Lady Rogers ruffled his hair in a daring way.

Sir Clifford snuggled her close. Not long after, she pushed away, her face flaming. "Cliffie," she said, shocked, "*not* in the breakfast room!"

Later that day, Phillida took up an argument Lord John had hoped was settled: ". . . But there is no need to continue our charade, my lord."

Lord John sighed. "Are we back to that?"

"You know we didn't agree."

"I didn't mean *that. Why,* love-o'-my-life," asked Lord John with pretended patience, "have I reverted to being 'my lord'?"

"Oh, very well. Lucas. But don't you see?"

"I see you are spoiling a perfectly lovely day."

He nodded to a passing matron, but continued

strolling with Phillida in such a possessive manner that no one dared approach them. Adroitly, he led them toward the river and a small coppice of beech trees. They were leaving behind the picnic party which had gathered in Richmond Park and, he hoped, would soon have some much-wished-for privacy. Not that he'd expected to use such a rare opportunity for *conversation*, but, if she insisted on this argument, then it was still a good thing to remove themselves from the others to where they might speak more openly with no fear of being overheard.

"Do be serious," she suggested, smiling at Lady Gwendolyn, who was walking on Mr. Diggory's arm. "Have you noticed Lady Gwendolyn no longer stands in that odd way?"

Lord John shrugged.

"The love of a good man has done her a world of good, I think," Phillida added.

"Why hasn't it done you any good?"

"Lucas," she reproved, spots of color glowing in her cheeks, "there is no need to flirt with me when no one can overhear."

He sighed. The day was *not* going well. "I'll be serious. Now tell me why you think we should end our engagement."

"Mother married Sir Clifford. I doubt she ever worried about my spinster status. That notion was just one of my aunt's little plots to trap me for poor Osbourn. So you see, there is no need for me to marry."

"Ah, but you forget, Philly, m'love." He noted her quick frown but ignored it. "We were supporting each other in our little game. I, too, must be protected from manipulative relatives. Remember?"

Phillida's mood lightened a great deal. "I did forget, didn't I?"

"There is, of course, the question of whether you've

found another man in whom you think you might take a serious interest."

"And you. Have you found a woman you'd care to pursue in earnest?"

"I asked first."

Phillida chuckled. "This could develop into a guessing game, each of us trying to assess the other's true feelings. I'll tell you frankly: I've met no man since meeting you with whom I think I could live my life."

"That sets me down finely, doesn't it?"

"You're flirting again."

"Am I?"

"Please? Be serious for just a moment longer?"

"Hmmm."

"*Have* you met someone?" She bit her lip. "I mean someone other than that lady who wouldn't have you?" Phillida touched his arm consolingly. "She must be a very strange lady, I think, to give you the go-by."

"Thank you for those kind words, Phil." She smiled, and he pinched her finger where it lay on his arm. He eyed her speculatively for a moment, then went on. "At the moment I fear to put it to the touch, so I'd appreciate it if you'd continue as my fiancée. My mother has hinted she'll soon return to the country. Our charade needn't be for much longer, if that worries you."

"Not at all. I'll gladly help as much as I can, as long as I can." Phillida drew in a deep breath, fearing she'd been too intense. "That's what friends are for, I think," she said, defusing what might become a dangerous moment if he'd understood her true feelings too well.

After a pause, he asked, "We *are* friends, are we not?"

"I certainly hope so."

"So do I, Phillida. I'd miss having you to talk to very much indeed."

They walked on in silence, turning eventually, without either seeming to give a signal, to stroll back toward

the others. Just in sight of the first group Lord John put
his arm around her shoulders, pulling her close for an
instant. He dropped a whisper of a kiss on the top of her
head and then pretended to notice that Mr. Merryweather was pointing them out to the others.

He believed Phillida had taken no notice of his newest
ploy to mark her as his own. There had been far too
many men, *interesting* men, gathering about her at social functions, and, if he didn't do something, someone
among them might catch her fancy. Word would spread
he'd kissed her. Given the odd way of it, gossip would
very likely change the story until it was unrecognizable.
It would be said they'd been seen in far greater intimacy
and he wouldn't care a whit. If he could get her no other
way, then perhaps he'd compromise her—not enough to
do permanent damage, just enough to force her to wed
him. Once he had her safe he'd teach her to love him.

Phillida was *not* oblivious to the little byplay. She
treasured the moment, only wishing it had been in private. Would he have really kissed her? If they'd been
alone? It was becoming something of an obsession with
Phillida that, before their sham engagement ended, she
experience his kiss. She desperately wanted the memory of it when she'd see him no more.

That evening the whole world could be found at the
Lievens'. Lord John escorted his mother and, as soon as
possible, found her particular cronies with whom he left
her. He searched the rooms twice before Merryweather
told him he'd observed Sir Clifford's party arriving only
moments earlier and that they were in the first an-
techamber. Lady Brookhaven was lecturing the new
Lady Rogers and, added Merryweather slyly, Sir Clifford was not quite succeeding in hiding his irritation.

Lord John thanked him for the information and hurried to find his love.

His own analysis of Sir Clifford's emotions led him to believe they were well beyond irritation. The man was steaming. Because they were in public he restrained himself, but it wasn't easy. Obviously. Before Lucas approached near enough to overhear what Lady Brookhaven said, he himself was accosted.

"Lord Brookhaven," he said, allowing his hand to be wrung.

"Thank you for introducing us that day." Brookhaven was accompanied by his new acquaintance of the Agricultural Society. "We've discovered so much in common, and I've met others who are interested in the things which interest me. I'm enjoying London for the first time ever. Thank you, thank you. If there is anything, *anything at all . . .*"

Lord John glanced again at the group which was *his* only interest at the moment and which he wished to join. He discovered he hadn't the heart to snub Osbourn, but he interrupted the younger man's effusion: "Are you, after all, making plans to take your seat in the House of Lords?"

Lord Brookhaven flushed. "I'm thinking of it. There are agricultural problems the nation must face. Serious problems. Don't suppose I'd make much difference, but I'd be of some trifling help if I voted the proper way."

"Excellent. Very proper. Now, I suspect Phillida is about to go on the warpath, as the red Indians are said to call it. I think we must interfere before our families become still another *on dit,* do you not?"

Lord Brookhaven looked, blanched, and would have turned tail if Lord John hadn't taken his arm.

"I doubt," said Osbourn, holding back, "I can do anything."

"We'll try. Chin up, my buck."

Lord Brookhaven had never been treated with such camaraderie by anyone half so tonish. He felt a small glow warming him. Symbolically he girded himself by pulling his coat more firmly onto his stocky shoulders and, after a word to his friend, allowed himself to be led into the fray.

"Good evening, Lady Brookhaven. You are keeping well? Lord Brookhaven tells me he is to take his seat in the Lords. Aren't you proud of him?"

Lord John's words interrupted Lady Brookhaven's low-voiced diatribe about unfeeling, disloyal, and disobedient nieces—of whichever generation. She sputtered, her thoughts jerked sideways to still another grievance. "He'll do no such thing. We need another Tory on the back benches as much as we need an English version of the French revolution."

Lord Brookhaven groaned and attempted to back away. He was held steady by Lucas's hand on his shoulder. "You're wrong, m'lady," said Lord John firmly. "Every peer should do his duty, whatever his politics. Lord Brookhaven will be an addition to the Lords with his special knowledge."

"Special knowledge! You jest." Lady Brookhaven's ire was turned completely on Lord John now. At first the others enjoyed the relief, but then they wondered how *they* might rescue *him*.

"Lady Brookhaven, there is more to government than foreign policy, whatever you Whigs think at the moment. As do many of the Tories, for that matter. The whole of Europe will very likely be affected before Napoleon is finally brought to heel, but that means some must keep their sights firmly here at home—or we *might* find the populace rising. Members like your grandson will do that. Their love of our country will see we do not ruin *it* while spending time and energy guarding Europe. I beg your pardon," he finished ruefully, his eyes straying around the interested, if shocked, group surrounding them. "How, I wonder, did I become so serious at what was a delightfully frivolous entertainment? Come, Phillida." He held out his arm and, when she laid trembling fingers on it, he looked to Sir Clifford and his lady. "I wish to introduce Phillida to my mother. Will you join us?"

"Oh, dear," whispered Lady Rogers. She looked to her husband for rescue, but he—foolishly, she thought—nodded and offered her his arm.

Sir Clifford bent near to her. "Stiffen your backbone, m'dear," Lord John heard him say to her. "Lady John can do nothing outrageous while here in a crowd. It is a marvelous generalship on Lord John's part, I think."

Lucas glanced at Phillida. She had overheard and was looking up at him, a pink patch on each cheek warning him she was embarrassed. "It seems to me," he mused, "that it might be as well if both sides of the family do their worst tonight. That way half the *on dits* will concern your aunt and the other half my mother, and then we may have a delightful hour soothing each other's ruffled feathers. I'll find it such fun soothing yours, m'dear," he finished on a note that raised her color still more but for quite different reasons.

"You, my lord, are a devil."

"Hmmm. You, my lass, are no angel."

"True," she riposted, regaining her equilibrium, "but, compared to you, I'm no more than an apprentice imp."

His brows rose in query. "My dear, to whom do you think you've been apprenticed? A very long apprenticeship, I hope?"

She chuckled, but, once again, he'd put her off balance. What was he implying? Or was it merely the sort of teasing she should ignore?

Phillida wished he'd thought of another way of breaking up the group which Lady Brookhaven had dominated—not that she wasn't pleased he'd done so before Sir Clifford or herself said something unforgivable . . . for, despite Lady Brookhaven's domineering ways, she was not evil. Her manipulations *were* based in a wish to do her family good. That she was wrongheaded was her only fault. Having escaped *her* family's private disagreements, Phillida wasn't looking forward to facing Lord John's. Lady John would be no less intimidating than Lady Brookhaven, and far less benign.

"Mother, I have brought my betrothed as promised. Here, too, are her mother and her stepfather. Lady Rogers, may I introduce Lady John?"

The two ladies nodded. There was wariness on the part of Phillida's mother, and practiced condescension on Lady John's side.

"I believe you know Sir Clifford, Mother? It isn't proper, of course, to bring him to your notice next, but I'm saving the best 'til last."

There was a murmur of soft chuckles from those listening. No one was disinterested in how Lady John would greet her future daughter-in-law. Sir Clifford bowed over Lady John's hand, his eyes never leaving hers. Lady John read a warning there and quite literally gnashed her teeth.

"And now, my love"—Lord John drew Phillida near, his arm lightly around her—"I present you to my ladymother. Mother, my wife-to-be, Miss Morgan, the future Lady John." He shouldn't have added that last—and knew it instantly it was done. His words added tinder to the embers of resentment which smoldered at all times in Lady John's breast. Phillida's advent into his life had fueled feelings which now burst into flames with the public reminder his marriage would depose her forever from her position of power, and, an added insult, force her to add the hated term *dowager* to her title.

Phillida curtsied. She, too, faced Lady John firmly,

not dropping her gaze or pretending a demureness which wasn't part of her character. Her color faded at the hatred she saw.

The haughty dame somehow looked down her nose at Phillida, even though she remained seated. "So. You've done well by yourself, have you not, missy?"

"Mother!" hissed Lord John. "I'm immodest enough I hope she feels she's done well, but not," he added, determined to keep things from developing into a scene, "so well as I've done. Phillida is all any man could wish in his wife. She is kind, loving, intelligent—not the typical empty-headed miss so common these days. In all ways, she is perfect for me. I never thought to find a woman with whom I could share so much." He smiled down at Phillida.

"Bah."

Lord John's lips thinned. "Have I mentioned the ship which leaves for the islands early next month, Mother? Should I arrange—"

"I am delighted to meet you. All of you," interrupted Lady John. "However, I find I am suffering a megrim and must depart. Lord John must order our carriage immediately."

"Of course," said her dutiful son. "Come, Phillida. We'll put Mother into her carriage and return to the party. As she *always* tells me, she will do much better with no one fussing her. You see, for many years all my efforts to aid her when she felt ill were thrown back in my face. I was, eventually, forced to believe her."

Lord John led Phillida away, his mother fuming on his other arm, but she attempted no more set-downs. They saw her into the carriage and stood by as it pulled away. "Well," said Lord John, pretending to mop sweat from his brow, "what an expedient headache. I wondered, for a moment, how to get her away from you."

"Why did you introduce us at all? We could have

avoided it somehow between now and when we end this farce."

"I thought it went rather well. I deliberately did it with a great crowd of people around us so it could not develop into just the sort of scene my mother delights in making."

"She hates me."

He chuckled, thinking she deliberately exaggerated. "Oh, nothing so desperate, I'm sure. Hate is so melodramatic."

"Lucas, I saw it in her eyes. She hates me. I'm not exaggerating." Phillida shuddered.

Lucas put an arm around her and drew her close. They couldn't stay out long. Also, the Lievens' butler stood framed in the open door watching them, which allowed him no freedom to soothe her agitation in the way he wished to do. His Philly was flustered by meeting his mother, obviously, but, if only he had a moment or two, surely he could bring her to a more moderate frame of mind. As he led her inside he held her arm close to his side, his hand over hers.

"You've faced too much tonight," he soothed. "It's over now, love."

Phillida heard condescension in his voice. It was his mother to whom she referred, and, she realized, he *couldn't* believe her statement.

"There you are," said Sir Clifford. He looked around, leaned forward, and said softly, "I rather wondered if Lady John had pulled out a pistol from that oversize reticule of hers and shot my brand-new daughter dead."

Lord John's brows rose.

"I've never seen anyone look at another person as your mother did at my daughter." Lady Rogers shuddered slightly and gave Sir Clifford a grateful look when he put his arm around her waist.

They *all* felt that way? "I must have missed something," said Lord John slowly. "I thought Philly—"

"Don't call me that."

"—was making it up and wondered if Sir Clifford was prone to making nasty jokes, but if you, all *three*, believe . . . No. Surely you exaggerate."

"Your mother hates me," repeated Phillida softly.

"Hate?" He shook his head, the rather condescending smile hovering around his mouth.

"Because you live on an even keel, my lord, you've no understanding of the darker, more dangerous, emotions." Lady Rogers paused, looking for supporting arguments. "Think, Lord John, have you ever been in a rage?"

"Very recently." His lips firmed. "When I discovered my interfering mother sent that last retraction to the papers, I experienced the strongest anger I've ever felt."

"But even then, your temper was not ungovernable, was it?" Phillida's mother sighed and shook her head. "There will be no convincing you of the necessity, but, even though you don't understand why, will you watch your mother, my lord? I don't wish anything to happen to my daughter. And from the look in her eye tonight, I think that woman capable of anything."

Lord John looked from one to the other. "Anything? You mean you fear she might try to *hurt* Phillida? Physically?" He read it in their eyes. They believed it. "Nonsense!"

"Not she herself, of course. She'd hire someone."

"Utter nonsense," repeated Lucas still more firmly.

"My lord, however demented we sound, we are not prone to falling into distempered freaks," said Sir Clifford softly. He hoped no one could overhear what was being said. They'd been so worried, no one had thought to wait until they had more privacy. "Just have someone keep an eye on her?"

Lord John fumed. He knew his mother was interfering and overly fond of getting her own way, but this was ridiculous. Nevertheless, he'd come to respect Sir Clifford, and his usually self-possessed Phillida was trembling. "I'll have her watched by someone I can trust," he promised, reluctantly.

"Thank you."

The evening continued predictably, even to Lord John leaving somewhat before Sir Clifford and his party. He was off, he told Phillida, to White's, where he was engaged for a hand or two of cards. To his surprise, he was actually glad to take his leave of her. He couldn't quite like the promise he'd made. To put a spy on one's mother! It was absurd to think her capable of anything more vicious than the use of her tongue—not that that couldn't be quite vicious enough, of course.

Now he wished to forget for a while. Tomorrow would be soon enough to set all in motion. It was very nearly a relief when his friends greeted him with ribald comments concerning his off-and-on engagement. One man suggested he'd been called to heel, that he'd live under the cat's paw. The notion jolted him, although he passed it off lightly enough. But the idea he could no longer call his life his own jabbed another needle into his uneasy conscience. Surely he hadn't made that promise because Phillida had some extraordinary hold over him, had he? Love didn't do that to one, did it?

An acquaintance Lord John could have done without joined their table. The play began, conversation dropping to no more than the occasional comment relevant to the progress of the betting. Finally, someone called for a new deck in the hopes it would change his luck and someone else took the opportunity to turn his coat inside out for the same reason. Everyone settled back with a round of hock or port or a rather fine, if very heavy, burgundy.

"When may we expect another announcement, Lord John?" asked the latecomer to the party, his sneer more obvious than normal. "We'll have nothing to gossip about if you settle into a perfectly normal engagement. Surely you're not planning we should die of ennui, are you?" The thin, graying man slouched back into his chair tossing a guinea and catching it in a habitual manner, the sneer reverting to a more normal sardonicism.

Lord John forced his features to show nothing of his irritation. "Another notice, Halbertson? There will be one more, of course." Eyebrows rose questioningly. "The one announcing our marriage." There were chuckles and groans around the table, indicative of which way various men had laid bets on the possibility they would actually get to the altar.

"Can you," asked Halbertson softly, "be certain there will be no others? If it's true, as is said, that you had nothing to do with the preceding retractions, how can you guarantee there will be no more?"

"He's right," chuckled one of Lucas's closer friends. "I myself could send in a notice the engagement was off again, and what's to stop me?"

For an instant Lord John's lips tightened dangerously, but he controlled his temper. "The fact none will be printed unaccompanied by my seal," he said easily, a lazy smile adding just the proper tone to the news.

"That was an excellent move, my lord," said Halbertson just as lazily. "However," he added, the coin again glinting in the candlelight, "now the fact is known, I suggest you watch your back. A lot of money is riding on the two of you."

"Including your own, Halbertson?"

"Actually, no." The coin rose, sparkled, turned, and fell back to his hand. "I arrived in town too late. Just as well, since it appears I'd have lost. I'd have bet against a marriage with the little Morgan. She's well enough, I suppose, but I'd not have thought she could hold you."

"Miss Morgan's name is to be left out of this and any other discussion, Halbertson. I'll not have her name bandied about the clubs."

Halbertson hooted. His love of pushing poison into someone and watching the result was one of the reasons Lucas had never liked him. Now Lord John's brows rose in query and the viper rose again. "You're too late. The name is heard everywhere. You'll be dueling for a year and a day if you try to stop it now!"

"I've never believed dueling the answer to anything. Perhaps, instead, my friends will let it be known how much I dislike this news?"

Silence descended, broken by the man who had called for fresh cards. He made more noise than necessary unwrapping them, the crackle of paper loud in the silence. "Are we playing or talking? If talking, we'd better adjourn to another room. We're getting dark looks from other tables, m'friends."

They played. It was late when Lord John and his friend, Major Anthony Ayers, left White's to stroll home. Their hope the fresh air would clear their heads of the fumes of far too much alcohol was, of course, futile.

"You know something, Lucas?" asked the major, his voice slurring slightly. Lord John grunted. "That Halbertson. He may have something. There is more money than one might think riding on the outcome of your engagement. Some men may not be quite as honorable as you or I. Know what?" Again Lord John made a noise suggesting he was listening. "I think you better guard against trouble."

"My God," said Lord John, suddenly furious, "why cannot people leave me alone to live my own life?"

"Er . . . Lucas?"

"No, no, not angry with you, Tony. Just can't seem

to clear my head, and it goes round and round and first this and then that and I can't think. You know?"

"Er . . . no. Can't say I do." But Major Ayers found his head was clearing faster than he liked under the influence of his friend's obvious turmoil. "Care to tell me? Don't *have* to. No wish to pry. Only thought maybe I could be of help?"

Lord John sighed. "Don't do it. That's what I say. You take my advice, old friend, and don't ever do it. You really mustn't do it." He shook his head slowly, back and forth.

"It?" asked his friend cautiously.

"Don't fall in love," said Lord John so sadly Major Ayers had to restrain a laugh. "It's a fool's game, this falling-in-love business."

That settled one question which had been plaguing the major ever since the first announcement. His fear Lord John had started some ploy he'd been caught in was obviously wrong. He pushed that notion out of his mind and concentrated on this new one. "I don't think that's true, Lucas. Think sometimes things don't always go well at the beginning, but once you get it sorted, then you're to be envied."

"You think so?"

"Wouldn't say it if I didn't believe it."

"Never really knew a love match personally," mused Lucas. After a pause he added, "Not to watch, you know."

"I have. My parents. And m'sister. Want it for myself."

"But you don't understand, ol' friend. She don't love me."

"You told her you love her?"

"Course not."

"Then how can she tell you she loves you? She's a

lady, ain't she? A lady can't be first saying those honored words, however unfair that is."

"You mean I have to bare m'soul to her without knowing if she'll laugh in m'face?"

"That's it."

Lord John, who had drunk far more than he was used to doing these days, let the idea seep through his sodden wits. "Won't work. She'll only think I'm telling taradiddles, playing the honorable part. She'll assume I'm doin' it 'cause I can't see any way out of this mess."

"Mess?" Worry returned with a rush, and Major Ayers eyed his friend with narrowed eyes.

Lord John yawned, his mind off on another tangent. "Mess? What mess? Why do you think I need watch my back?"

Major Ayers was no longer so well-to-go as Lord John since he'd involuntarily sobered, but his friend's question confused him. "Watch your back?"

"Yes. You said there'd be trouble."

"Trouble. With your engagement?"

"Anthony, pay attention now. You said there was pots of money on it. You said there'd be trouble. Why?"

"Oh. Someone with money on the breakup of your engagement will get the notion that another notice will do the trick—to save his groats, you know. But you let the cat out of the bag when you said another notice wouldn't be accepted without your seal. So someone will get the bright idea he should steal the seal. Trouble."

"Oh."

"That all you can say?"

"Thought you meant my mother."

"Why should I . . . Oh. So she sent one notice, did she? Guessed as much."

"Didn't mean that. Just seems everyone thinks my

mother will cause trouble. Don't want to spy on my mother."

Anthony's bewilderment grew. Then he remembered what Lady John was like. "Spy on your mother?" He nodded portentously. "Very good notion, that."

"You, too?" Lord John sighed.

"Me, too." Major Ayers thought about that. "Me and who else?"

"Phillida says m'mother hates her. Like in a farce. Didn't think my little Philly would act that way."

Major Ayers, about to support Phillida's belief, was once again sidetracked. "Filly? You call Miss Morgan a *filly?* Don't think she'd like that, Luke."

"Not a *filly.* Philly. Short for Phillida." Lord John had never thought of the pun. He finally saw why Phillida didn't like the nickname. A chuckle formed, grew. "Filly! She thought I was calling her a filly!"

The major sighed, took his friend by the arm, and stuffed him into the hackney he halted for the purpose. It seemed a good idea to take Lucas to his lodgings and put him to bed on the couch. Then, in the morning, once their heads were clear, the two of them could sift through all the bits and pieces his friend had hinted at tonight.

Ten

Tuttles headed straight for the settle inside the ancient fireplace where, as usual, Porterman sat, his toes extended toward a small fire. "I can't stay," said Tuttles, waving off the barmaid.

"Not for so much as a half-pint?" Porterman noticed his friend's worried expression and, painfully, straightened. "What is it?"

"Lady John sent for that groom last night—the one she saved from transportation? You remember?"

The story was not a pleasant one, concerning, as it did, revenge and the daughter of a coachman, the girl's disfigurement, and subsequent suicide. In one sense, however, Lady John had been right: there'd been no hint of more trouble concerning the groom.

"So?"

"Lady John left early this morning for the country."

"Tutt, old friend, is there a point?"

"The groom remained behind."

"Did he now?"

"Over there. The small one by the door in the beat-up old tricorn hat and the dirty livery."

"That isn't Lord John's livery."

"No, it isn't. Which does nothing to ease my suspicions. At first I thought maybe she'd come to her senses and booted him, but according to his lordship's head groom, we're still to house the little tick."

"Sullen sort o' chap," said Porterman thoughtfully, eyeing the newcomer to the tavern.

"No one likes him, so I expect he'll spend his time here. I'm not suggesting you take him up—that horse won't run because he's sure to notice you and I are friends—but if you could set someone onto him? Try and find out *why* he's stayed behind?"

"Bitsey'll be in later," Porterman said after a moment. The men's eyes met. Simultaneously, each nodded. "Bitsey can get information out of stone walls—when she's in the proper mood."

Porterman extended a hand. Tuttles laid a pair of golden boys in his friend's palm and watched ruefully as the money disappeared into his friend's pocket. "If my suspicion Lady John left that scum in London with orders to harm Lord John is true, I'll not feel I've wasted my money." He sighed. "I must run now."

Lord John raised one eyelid, noted a familiar crack zigging and zagging across the ceiling, and closed the eye with a groan. Why, he wondered, was he sleeping on Tony's lumpy sofa? He hadn't done that for months. Not, he decided after some difficult cogitation, since he'd stopped drinking London dry in an unsuccessful attempt to forget the horrors of bayonet warfare in the fog-shrouded battle at Bussaco, his last battle before he'd had to sell out.

Lord John opened the other eye to see if it saw the same thing. Definitely Tony's ceiling. He moaned softly, his head swollen to twice its normal size, and, remembering Phillida's comments on swelled heads and hats, chuckled. It was an error. Immediately the swelling doubled. Lying very still, he waited for his head to return to something closer to normal—still outsize, but, by comparison, very nearly tolerable.

"Coffee?"

"You awake, Tony?"

"Not very. Not for long."

"Why'd I drink so much last night?"

"Think you were unhappy, Luke."

"Unhappy? Me?"

"Don't take me for a flat. Said something about Miss Morgan not loving you while you were head over heels with her."

"I said that?" Lord John opened one eye cautiously, watched his friend nod solemnly. He thought about it. "Can't have said any such thing," he decided. "Don't believe in being in love."

"Didn't say you were *in love*. Said you *loved*. Different thing. Loving lasts, but one can be in love over and over."

"You should know."

"We aren't talking about me," said Major Ayers with great dignity.

"Well, don't want to talk about *me*," replied Lucas.

"Coffee?" asked the major again.

Lord John chuckled, decided it was still an error to laugh, and very carefully sat up. Neither spoke until after they'd imbibed a couple of cups of the dark brew.

"Better?"

Lord John nodded. "Think I may live. Why do I do that?"

"It's been a while. Quite a while."

"My only consolation." Lord John thought back over the preceding evening. "Did what's-his-name say something about my being in danger?"

"Halbertson? Yes. Suggested someone might try to take your ring so they could use your seal to send a notice to the papers."

"Hmmm." Lord John's head rang with his effort to sort things out. "Don't think that's everything. Something else . . . something to do with Mother," he said finally.

Major Ayers nodded. "Made a promise."

Lord John sent his mind back further into the mists of memory, remembered the meeting between Phillida and his mother. He groaned. "Dammit, Tony. Women are irrational and men are fools."

The major's lips twitched, but he bit back a chuckle. "How so?"

"Phillida thinks my mother hates her and Sir Clifford fears Mother will do her damage." He sighed lugubriously. "I am, if you'll believe it, to put a spy on my mother to see she don't plan something dastardly."

"Good idea."

Lord John blinked. "You, too?"

"Lady John is an excessively selfish woman. She wants nothing to interfere with her position or her power. You know that."

"I do?"

"Why else did she push all those weak-willed brainless bits at you, telling you they'd make perfect wives?" He answered himself: "Knew she could control them, of course. Just like she did your sister-in-law. You don't think she could control Miss Morgan, do you?" Again he answered himself. " 'Course not. But your mother won't allow her position to be usurped by someone who will gather the reins into her own hand. So . . . what's she to do?" This time he left the question dangling.

Lord John pondered, then shook his head. "She's got a tongue on her which won't stop, but beyond lying to her cronies what can she do? And she won't do that now. I've got her tongue tied in knots. There's nothing she can do to hurt my Philly." Philly? Something wrong with that. "I mean my Lida."

"You put a muzzle on *Lady John?*"

Her son grinned. "Threatened to send her to the West

Indies to my uncle. He's as strong-willed as she is and wouldn't give her an inch. So my mother will behave herself here."

"What if something happens to Miss Morgan and you don't know she had a hand in it?"

"Tony, why have all my friends and acquaintances suddenly developed this streak of melodrama? Never realized how many people had one."

"Luke, hate to upset you, but Lady John just isn't that innocent."

"She's a beldam if there ever was one. Never said she was innocent."

"I mean she'll do anything to get her way."

"What're you talking about?"

"Never told you. Didn't like to. Your *mother,* you know."

"No, I don't know what you have skittering around in your head."

"Come down off your high horse or I won't tell you now."

Lord John sighed. "I'm down." He stared straight ahead, not really wanting to hear his friend's story. Once it was over, he shook his head. "Not my mother."

"Why not your mother?"

"No one in the John family would behave in such a scaly way."

"Y'mother married into the family. Not part of it natural-like."

Lord John thought about that. "She told you that? What you said?"

"Yes."

"She thought you'd believe it?"

Major Ayers nodded.

"Why'd she do it?"

"I suppose to make me feel inadequate, unworthy to be your friend. In fact, she *said* I wasn't worthy."

"That doesn't explain it."

"She'd not managed to split us up any other way."

Lord John thought about that. "All you had to do was look in the mirror."

"Just a boy. Might not think of that until too late."

"So what *did* you do?"

"Went home and asked m'father."

Lord John winced. "That took courage."

"Lady John has never understood the power of love and respect. Had both for m'father, and he for me."

"So you actually asked him if you were your mother's illegitimate son whom he'd taken in, and if it were your brother who was really the heir?"

"Needed to know."

Lord John thought about what he'd heard. "But, Tony, that don't make her any worse than I've always known her to be."

The major shook his head. "Very vicious thing to do. Only a boy. Could have ruined m'whole life if I'd believed her."

Lord John adopted a mulish expression.

"Look," said the major patiently. "She's y'mother and you want to think the best of her. Understand that. But you love Phillida. Don't want her hurt. So you balance that against this and decide what to do."

Lord John pushed himself up, his bloodshot eyes as sad as an old dog's. "No question when you put it that way."

"Well?"

"Got t'go home and arrange to have m'mother watched."

At home he discovered his mother had left town. Relief flooded him. He needn't compromise his moral sense by setting someone to spy on his mother. He took himself up to his bedroom and, after allowing Tuttles to help him from his coat and boots, dismissed the butler. He stripped down before crawling into the bed Tuttles had quietly turned down. He could get another three or four hours' sleep before he need show his nose anywhere.

"Well, Father?"

"Not so well, m'dear."

"Pain worse today?" Flint quietly ordered a ball of fire for her father, the gin as good a painkiller as anything available.

"Bit the worse, maybe. Damp does it to me. But 'tisn't that."

"Then what has you in the mopes?"

"Worried."

"Father," she said with what patience she could find. "I haven't all day." Her father, she knew, was dragging it out to keep her near—he was often lonely.

"Don't look now, but, easy-like, lay your glims on the bad lot in the corner near the door. Then you keep your peepers peeled for him and if he comes near your mistress, you do what you must to protect her."

"Are you making any sense?"

"Don't look at me as if I were gibbering and drooling. Tell you that man may be a danger to your Miss Morgan."

"I think you'd better tell me more than that."

Porterman explained. ". . . Didn't work. That candidate for a hangin' won't let anyone near him. If Bitsey couldn't discover nothing, no one could. Worse, she won't give back the yellow boy I gave her as earnest money and I can't give but the one back to Tutt. Don't like to say I failed him, daughter. Don't like to contradict Tuttles neither, but think the groom may be set to hurt your Miss Morgan rather than his Lord John like Tutt thinks. Makes more sense. Lady John wouldn't want to hurt her son."

Flint sorted through that. "You think the groom is to scar Miss Morgan as he did that coachy's daughter so that Lord John will cry off?"

Porterman sent his daughter a scornful look. "Lord John wouldn't." He lowered his nose a trifle and added, "But Miss Morgan might, thinking she was no longer an acceptable parti, don't you know?" Flint blenched. "Understand now?" She nodded. "So take a look at the man, syr-up-ti-tious-like. Maybe warn your miss danger's up and walking and *watch the shadows*."

Flint, taking care to peer from the depths of her bonnet, studied the man by the door. Sullen soul, she thought. Livery dirty and badly worn—but clothing could be changed. She needed something which would identify the man under any condition. But he was so . . . so . . . such a nothing of a man.

"He's got a slight limp," said her father, as if reading her mind.

Flint nodded, watched a bit longer. "That left hand looks funny-like."

"Like a claw. Don't show much when he wears gloves, mind. The coachy broke his fingers into pieces after the slime hurt his daughter."

"Good for him. I'm afraid there is nothing which will make him stand out in a crowd, but I'll do my best. That weak chin is one thing, and the broken nose." She sighed. "You say he scarred the girl's face?"

"Hearts on her cheeks—as if they'd been lovers, you know? Wasn't true. No wonder she drowned herself, is it?"

"And Lady John saved him from transportation? Why?"

"Said he'd been sadly provoked."

"Nothing should provoke one to that sort of revenge. The coachman may, for all I know, have deserved it, but the coward took it out on a defenseless girl. If he'd carved up the coachman, now . . . But even then I'd not want the man anywhere near *me*."

"There was only one denial in that last batch of responses, Mother."

"I'd no notion my Cliffie knew so many people." Lady Rogers's hand trembled.

"No need to be nervous. Entertaining in London is exactly the same as at home—only more so. There will be plenty of Miss Fairfaxes and Mr. Trouts and Lady Percys and Sir Richards and a large gaggle of young girls looking for husbands and young men whose mothers want them married. Just the same."

Lady Rogers laughed as her daughter intended, and pretended horror. "Not a Lady Percy. Say not!"

"At least two," said her unrepentant daughter with a grin. "Just as picky and just as foolish—and just as easily ignored."

"Easy for you to say," said her mother, "but I never could ignore our Lady Percy as you did. Now I'm more nervous than ever. Have you dealt with the caterers, Phillida?" she asked, lifting a list from the pile stacked beside her luncheon plate.

"Yes. *And* with the dealer in blooms *and* hired link boys to see to the traffic *and* checked the awning, which, by the way, needs a new cover, which I've ordered. What do you wish me to do today?"

"Would you care to take up the carpet in the drawing room?" asked her mother, deadpan.

Phillida pretended to think it over. "No, I think not. I'd hate to deprive you of such a delightful task, you see." She eyed her mother. "Are you really lifting it? I doubt it has been up since it was laid."

"Exactly. And yes. It comes up today."

"How many footmen will that take?"

"I'll find out, won't I?"

Her mother looked as though it was all a big joke, but Phillida couldn't help but be relieved when a note was brought to her informing her that Lord John found it necessary to inspect the damage caused by a recent storm to the roofs at one of his minor, but quite delightful, estates. He'd thought to combine duty with pleasure and was inviting his cousin, Mrs. Greenmont, Lady Gwendolyn, and his friend, Major Anthony Ayers, for a picnic on the manor grounds. He'd be delighted if Phillida would join him on the jaunt, and if she'd care to propose additions to the party.

"Excuse me, Mother. I must answer this immediately."

Phillida's response suggested that Mr. Diggory be added.

It was a pleasant drive once they'd passed beyond the markets and through the poor district on the south side of the Thames. The tree-covered hills gentled into fields with tall hop poles. Hump-topped oasthouses dotted the countryside. In the orchards the blossoms had been replaced by young fruit. And, of course, there were occasional neat villages, the thatched-roofed cottages lining both sides of the road. To make the day perfect, there was laughter and good fellowship and the anticipation of an *al fresco* meal.

Upon their arrival Lord John designated Major Ayers as host while he went with his factor to inspect the damage. Mrs. Greenmont, who had been there often, showed the others around the well-kept grounds.

"You'd never know there'd been a storm, would you?" asked Phillida.

Mayor Ayers disagreed. "You say that because you don't know the manor, Miss Morgan. *You* noticed, did you not, Cressy?"

"Yes," said Mrs. Greenmont. "It is sad, isn't it? But

you haven't a notion of what we speak, have you, Miss Morgan? Lucas didn't mention the loss of the ancient tree which sheltered Charles the Second?"

"Not another one!"

"Yes, another one," said the major. I think every surviving tree of that period has a history of having sheltered Old Rowley on his escape from England. But I warn you, Lucas and I used to play at Roundheads and Cavaliers, and neither of us wishes to hear a word against our particular tree—except, of course, it is gone."

"It was a beautiful old oak, Miss Morgan," explained Mrs. Greenmont. "We can see where it once stood if we walk that direction. There," she added after a moment, and pointed to where gardeners smoothed the earth. They strolled closer, and Major Ayers spoke with the head gardener.

"Why don't we plant a new one?" asked Phillida as they waited for him.

"What?" asked Major Ayers, half hearing.

"Why don't we," repeated Phillida, "ask the gardener to find a young oak which we might help plant to replace the one which blew down. It won't be the same. Nothing could be. But it would commemorate a lovely day in the country and could remind one of the tree which once stood there. Or should we first ask Lord John?"

"What a thoughtful suggestion," said Mrs. Greenmont. "I like the notion excessively, and so will Lucas." She looked at the gardener, who, ignoring the women, stared at the major. "Anthony, I believe you'll have to make the request."

Major Ayers did so, and the gardener nodded. "Know just the tree, Major," he said, his Kentish accent so broad that Phillida had difficulty following.

"Well then, dig it up and have it here by"—the major

looked at his watch, snapped it shut, and replaced it—
"oh, by two, I think?"

The gardener nodded. He hesitated, then turned toward Phillida and, his eyes averted, made a funny jerky
bow and stalked off.

"Well." Mrs. Greenmont stared after the bent old
man.

"Well, indeed." Major Ayers's eyebrows arced high.
"You've made a conquest, Miss Morgan."

"I have?"

"Definitely. I've never before seen the old grouch
admit to the existence of a female."

Phillida laughed. "He didn't then—he only honored
my idea!"

The picnickers started home in good time, planning
to stop for refreshment at a pretty inn on the Thames
which the gentlemen thought the ladies would enjoy. It
required their taking a different route from the one they
had driven out on, which took them to the west, but no
one objected to the longer journey because no one particularly wanted the delightful day to end. They were
approaching the first really bad grade—long rather than
steep—when an errant breeze caught Mrs. Greenmont's
parasol and swung it away into the nearby meadow.
"Oh, do stop," she called to the driver. "I searched forever to find just that shade of rose."

The coachman pulled to the side and one of the
grooms obligingly hopped down from the back of the
carriage. While he chased after the parasol—which
the wind continually tossed just beyond his reach—the
men gathered around to tease Mrs. Greenmont.

Suddenly, sweating horses and a heavy coach pulled
over the brow of the hill. It was instantly obvious the
team raced out of control. Someone blew a weak tattoo
on the yard of tin and Lucas's spirited team, well trained
as it was, decided to take offense. They reared, backed,

Jeanne Savery

and started forward, startling everyone. Before the coachman could control them, they jerked the carriage once again and the rear axle cracked, a wheel slanting into the roadway. It all seemed to happen in an instant.

Lord John and the major flicked each other a glance, nodded instant understanding, and set their mounts up the hill toward the runaways. Swearing, the coachman cut at the traces—the footman helping him when he could tear his eyes from approaching disaster. The women had been thrown to one side of the carriage when the wheel broke. They untangled themselves, and Mr. Diggory hurriedly lifted them out and away from the roadway, which, all too soon, was expected to be a scene of chaos.

Mr. Diggory held Lady Gwendolyn. She sobbed softly, her head hidden against his shoulder and neck. Mrs. Greenmont, dazed—having hit her head rather hard—leaned against a tree. Phillida knew she should attend the woman, but couldn't take her eyes from Lord John.

The men rode to either side of the oncoming team. The maneuver they then executed gave Phillida nightmares for weeks. Somehow they were no longer on their own mounts, but had transferred to the backs of the lead horses of the runaway team. They leaned forward, caught the reins, pulled back. Phillida held her breath. Could they do it? It was a long hill, but the coach was old and heavy and awkwardly designed. Why had no one thrown out the drag which would help them slow? And the brake. Was the brake broken?

In the meantime, the coachman worked demonically to release Lord John's team. The first animal was freed and the driver smacked its flank; the animal objected to such treatment but moved into the ditch nevertheless. Another followed almost immediately, and then the runaways, slowed now, were nearly upon them. The driver pulled the wheel team to the side, while the footman, mouth open, gaped at the fast-approaching coach.

One of the runaways reared, dragging its teammate with it, and Phillida feared Lucas and the major would be thrown. Cursing, each brought his animal under control. Trembling and sweating, the team stilled.

Sitting on the box were two very young and very frightened lads. Lord John looked from one to the other. He looked at the frightened women, his damaged carriage—at which he frowned for an instant—and back at the pair of would-be whips who had, at a minimum, very nearly broken their own necks as well as endangered Lord John's party. His scowl deepened.

"Careful, Luke," said Major Ayers. "Remember Brighton in 'ninety-three."

Lord John's eyes widened. He turned and stared at his friend. They burst into laughter. The culprits on the runaway carriage looked at each other. Weakly, they, too, laughed, although they hadn't a notion why. Reminded of his own grass-time idiocy, Lord John left Ayers to scold the lads. "Is everyone all right?" he asked, approaching his guests.

"Except for my heart stopping my throat so I'll not be able to eat for a week, I suppose I'm all right," responded Mrs. Greenmont, a tart note adding acid to her tone.

Phillida, finally able to tear her gaze from Lord John, turned to Mrs. Greenmont, who, she discovered, had slid down to sit on the ground. Her head was laid back against the tree, and she had her eyes closed.

Concerned, Phillida knelt next to her. "Are you hurt?"

"Merely sending up a prayer of thanks that all is well. When Lucas and Tony decided to out-Astley Sergeant-Major Astley, I swear I feared the worst. *Now* I feel like scolding them for playing such a trick."

"If they had not, those boys would very likely be lying in the road with their necks broken."

"True enough," Mrs. Greenmont added, still a trifle acidly. "But such stupidity deserves more than to be rewarded with a good story with which to regale all their friends who will take them for heroes instead of the idiots they actually are."

Mr. Diggory, his arm supporting Lady Gwendolyn, opportunely approached. "Let me congratulate you and the major on such quick action. I dread to think what might have happened if the two of you weren't so capable. Come, Gwendolyn, dear, we'll carry our words of approbation further and, perhaps, save those young hellions a mite of the scolding the major is handing out to them." He led her toward the road.

"I thought *you'd* read those boys their lesson," said Mrs. Greenmont.

Lord John grinned ruefully. "I can't."

"Why not?" asked Phillida.

"Anthony reminded me of the time I pulled much the same stunt with rather worse result. There was no one around to save me from folly, you see."

"Thus you leave the scold to the major. I see."

"M'lord?" The coachman stood by, hat in his hand.

"Yes, Matthews?"

The driver scowled ferociously. "Want you ta see somethin', m'lord."

Lord John exchanged a deep look with the graying man. "Excuse me, ladies. I'd best go with Matthews for a moment."

"What," said Phillida, "do you suppose that is all about?"

"I haven't a notion. Help me up and let's go see."

Phillida and Mrs. Greenmont quietly followed to where the coachman was pointing to the broken axle.

". . . not natural-like, m'lord."

"I agree." Lord John's fierce look startled Phillida. When he looked at the women his eyes narrowed and he seemed to stare right through them. "Surely not," he said very nearly under his breath. "I'm developing as much imagination as everyone else." He turned back to his coachman. "Matthews, we'll need another carriage to convey the ladies home."

"Sent Joe back to that hedge tavern. Likely won't do no good, though. He's up on Brownie, m'lord, the only one of the four what'll tolerate a rider."

"If there is no suitable vehicle, I'll commandeer *that* one." Lord John stalked away to tell the thoroughly cowed young men they weren't to drive off.

Phillida looked after him and then back to the coachman. "Matthews, could you tell me what caused the damage to our carriage?"

"Nasty games, like." His perpetual scowl deepened. "Didn't think. Might a hurt the horses."

Overhearing him, Major Ayers spoke sternly. "You mean *the ladies* might have been hurt." Matthews didn't contradict him, but he obviously didn't agree. The major stared at Miss Morgan. "*Are* you all right?"

"Me?" asked Phillida. "Oh. You mean all of us."

"No, I don't. I'm pretty certain it was *you* who was meant harm." Phillida looked startled. Major Ayers sighed. "Shouldn't have said anything, Miss Morgan. Wouldn't have, except I believe I must put you on your guard."

Matthews was still worried about his horses. "I'll have me words with a certain lowlife and we'll see what the nasty little insect has to say for hi'self. Then we'll know, won't we?"

"Are you, too, saying someone wished to hurt me?" Phillida asked him.

"Could a hurt the horses," repeated the coachman as he stalked off.

Phillida looked at Mrs. Greenmont, then back at the major. "I insist you explain what you mean."

"Haven't a shred of proof, Miss Morgan, so I don't think I can. But I think you should watch for trouble." He stared at the broken axle.

Bemused, Phillida also stared. Then she shook her head. She joined Lady Gwendolyn, who looked a trifle forlorn. "Were you hurt, after all?"

"Oh, no. It is just that it was such a wonderful day for me, and then to have something so awful happen! I mean," she blushed, "I hate for anything to spoil everyone's day." Gwendolyn looked toward where Mr. Diggory talked to one of the young men, and the blush deepened.

Phillida was no fool. She grinned. "How wonderful!" Phillida hugged Gwendolyn, who blushed still more. "I'll only wish you happy and won't say another word."

"I don't know how you guessed. We may not, with propriety, inform anyone until Mr. Diggory talks to my father." Gwendolyn giggled. "Assuming, of course, he can get Father's attention long enough to do so!"

"I'm so happy for you." But wishing her friend happy made her own engagement seem even more wrong. Feeling hopeless, Phillida wandered off to sit under the tree which had supported Mrs. Greenmont and waited patiently for their situation to sort itself out. Eventually they continued on their way home—where she thought she might indulge in just ten minutes' worth of self-pitying tears. No more. After all, tears were such a lamentable waste of time, and she'd sworn she'd not waste a minute of what she'd have with Lucas.

Eleven

Major Ayers studied the deviled veal offered him by Lord John's butler. He'd finished a nice little bird and was debating between the veal and a slice of ham. Unable to decide, he took both. Chewing thoughtfully, he eyed his friend and wondered if he should say anything on the subject of the broken axle. Undecided, he tiptoed toward it. "You're looking a trifle grim, old friend."

Lord John looked at Tuttles, who stood silently next to the laden buffet. He dismissed him and the footmen. The door closed behind his butler's stately back and the grim look deepened. "Sir Clifford was not at home when we left Phillida. I must talk to him, Tony. He must have an eye to her protection."

Major Ayers manfully put down his knife and fork.

Lord John, aware of his friend's prodigious appetite, chuckled. "No need to go this minute. My love stays in this evening. She'll be safe enough at home, so finish breaking your long fast before we track down Sir Clifford." He took a deep draft of wine—not his first—and the grim look returned. "If I could, I'd marry her out of hand. As it is, I've no right to be near her most of the day."

"So convince her."

"When we've not even got a real engagement," he growled, "how do you suggest I suddenly insist she marry me?"

"Tell her."

"That I love her? I haven't the nerve. She is constantly reminding me of the time when we'll end our game."

Major Ayers's chuckle brought Lord John's head up. "You won't admit there is nothing else she can do. You must let her know *you love her*."

"It won't wash, Tony. She'll merely accuse me of flirting—which is what she always does when I attempt to get closer to her."

The major swallowed another mouthful of ham dabbed with mustard sauce and reached for his wine. Put like that, he understood. "It's a problem."

Finished, they removed with the decanter, to the library. Silence reigned as they savored a very fine brandy with which Tuttles had recently and—his master feared—illicitly replenished his cellars. There were, he thought, some very awkward problems about the war—the supply of good brandy was one of them. He refilled their glasses, settled back, and cast a suspicious eye toward Major Ayers. He scowled. "You're laughing at me."

"Can't help it. Never thought to see Lucas Strathedene, the army's foremost lover, unable to bring a woman—any woman—around his thumb."

Spots of red glowed in Lord John's cheeks. "Not the same sort of woman, Tony. Besides, that's all in the past. Nothing to do with Phillida. Can't treat your bride like you would a mistress."

"She's a woman, ain't she?"

"No."

The major sat up with a jerk. "She *isn't?*"

"What?" Lord John absently refilled their glasses. "Of course she's a woman. But she's also a lady. There's a difference."

Major Ayers looked at his nails, studied them. "There isn't," he offered casually. "Not really."

"Tony . . ."

"It's true. There ain't any real difference. Tonish women have, underneath that training which hides them, all the feelings and emotions of the . . . well, the *other* sort."

Lord John eyed him suspiciously. "Where'd you get a notion like that?"

"M'mother. She wants me to treat my bride right."

"What bride?"

"Any bride." Major Ayers shrugged. Then he noted his friend's gaping mouth. "Not anytime soon. Just whenever."

Lord John's mouth closed and firmed into a stern line.

"Don't look so horrified. Tonish women don't go around looking for protectors, because they have men to look after them—fathers and brothers and husbands. That doesn't mean they can't enjoy . . . well, you know."

"So what are you suggesting?"

"Don't use that dangerous note on me." Major Ayers finished off his brandy and reached for the decanter. "You don't scare me, because I know you won't call me out."

He wore such an innocent look, Lord John laughed. "Are you going to tell me your notion?" he asked.

The major stared into his glass. "I wouldn't suggest you exactly seduce Miss Morgan."

"No," said Lord John, danger back in his voice. "I don't think you should suggest *that*." He remembered he himself had done so, once, when teasing her.

"But perhaps you could allow yourself a little leeway? Just enough she can't help knowing how you feel?"

Lord John ground his teeth, but the idea was firmly planted in his head. *Would* she respond to his advances? And if she did? The mere thought of Phillida in his arms, her skin under his hands, was making him feel—

all those things he couldn't talk about. Even with Tony. "How did we get off on such a subject?" he asked, his neck hot and his ears burning.

"Wasn't difficult. Merely suggested you sweep your Philly off her feet."

"Isn't a filly."

"Never said she was."

Two old friends glowered at each other—then burst out laughing.

Major Ayers dared to suggest, "Silly filly needs a strong hand."

"Philly isn't silly."

"Is if she isn't already in love with you."

"Seem to remember you saying there's a difference between loving and being *in* love."

"Is. But the one can grow out of the other. Being in love is easiest, and you'll have to admit a lot of women have felt that way about you."

"I don't admit any such thing."

Major Ayers gave him a sly look. "Bet you a monkey she's in love with you."

"You don't know my Lida."

"Strong-minded woman. I know."

"Independent," suggested Lord John.

"Hmm. Still. Bet you a monkey."

"One doesn't bet on a lady's affections. It isn't done." Major Ayers became stubborn. "Still . . ."

"Besides, how could such a wager be settled?"

An arrested look passed over the major's features. "Haven't a notion," he admitted.

Lord John shook his head in disgust. "What time is it?"

Major Ayers fumbled for his watch and managed to open it. He peered at the face. "I make it twelve thirty-three. Why?"

"Want to find Sir Clifford."

"Tonight?"

"He should know."

"So where does one start looking?" Major Ayers struggled up from the deep, comfortable chair. He sat back down. "Know what, Luke?"

"What?"

"Don't think I'm going much of anywhere. How often did you refill my glass there?"

Lord John rose to his own feet. His head spun. "Damned if I know."

"Said she was staying in. Ain't in danger tonight," suggested the major.

Lord John blinked, came to a decision. "I'll send a note around she's not to go out until I see her in the morning."

"Now that's good thinking, Luke," said Major Ayers admiringly, "for someone as foxed as you are."

"Who said I was foxed? Maybe a bit on the go. Not *quite* the thing, I suppose—but *not foxed*."

With great dignity and greater care, Lord John removed to his desk, where he scribbled a note to his love. A great blotch of ink obscured half his signature. He peered at it. He tried a second note with still less success and reread the first. It would do. He rang for a footman. When Bobs arrived, Lord John spoke to him in the manner of a man who doesn't want another to notice his condition. He was careful to make his orders perfectly clear—and in the process repeated himself thrice—adding unnecessary reminders that the lad hurry and others that he not wait for an answer, which he contradicted by the further instruction that Lord John wished to know if his love understood his message.

"Porterman, old friend, you remember Mr. Matthews, don't you? We've come looking for that groom." Tuttles waved over the saucy barmaid, who soon returned with three pints. "I'll let Matthews tell you what he told me." Tuttles looked around the room. "By the way, where *is* Lady John's man?"

Porterman extended his hand to Matthews before answering Tuttles's question. "Haven't seen him since yesterday. Problem?"

Matthews gently shook the painfully bent hand offered to him. "Need to find the scum. Don't know what it is about grooms these days."

Porterman looked politely but curiously at Tuttles. Tuttles raised his eyes to the ceiling and put his nose back into his mug. Porterman looked back at Matthews, who had settled comfortably and was enjoying the fire and his ale.

Tuttles, seeing irritation growing in Porterman, quickly summarized what had happened to Lord John's carriage. "We'd hoped to find Lady John's man here. Both of us want a few words with that . . . with him."

"You think he did something to the carriage?"

"When the party arrived in Kent, Matthews turned the team into a paddock. He tells me someone opened the gate to the far side of the field and all the horses—not just the team—were let out. Matthews had to help the reduced staff his lordship keeps down there get them back in. So the carriage was left alone for nearly an hour, you see. Who else would have done the damage?" The three men stared into the fire. Finally Tuttles asked, "I don't suppose the little rat was seen prowling around down there?"

"I've sent my best boy down to find out," said Matthews, unexpectedly rejoining the conversation. "Don't think he'll learn much of anything, though. Scum's slippery as an eel when he don't want no one to know what he's up to."

"Someone better find him," suggested Porterman.

"He can't be allowed to go around endangering whole coachloads of women."

"Little sod didn't think," said Matthews with heat. "Could have hurt the *horses*. Don't think we'll see the weasel again." Matthews finished his ale and belched. "Very good brew they have here, Mr. Tuttles. Thank you for the treat."

Porterman and Tuttles looked questioningly at each other. Matthews spent so much time with his horses, it was sometimes difficult getting him to make sense when talking to humans. "What makes you think the man has disappeared?"

"Not stupid. Has to."

"*I* must be stupid. Why does he have to?"

"Showed his hand."

"No, he hasn't. Not unless someone saw him."

"Don't need proof. He knows I know. Knows I'll beat his ears off for putting that team in jeopardy."

"Matthews has no daughter, so that's all right . . ." Tuttles and Porterman grinned at each other. But there was no convincing Matthews that people were more important than his four-legged charges. "What do we do now?" asked Tuttles.

"M'daughter knows to watch over Miss Morgan. What else is there?" The three men stared into the fire. Finally Porterman added, "Makes you feel sort of helpless-like, don't it?"

Phillida read the note. She read it again. There was something in the careful formation of letters marred by spluttering drops of ink which bothered her. Finally she figured it out. Lucas was cast away. He was so far up in his altitudes he would never remember he'd written her, let alone the note's content. She told Rutgers, who stood by waiting for an answer, that there would be no return message.

Phillida read the note once more: "Dear Philly" was crossed out and followed by: "My dear Lida, love of my life, treasure of my heart, do not, I beg you, leave the house until I come to you on the morrow. Please? Don't do it? Not even into the garden in the square. Not if you love me at all?"

Finally, it was signed "Strathedene" rather than "Lucas" or "Luke." Not so much as a "faithfully yours"—which, of course, he wasn't. Of course, there wasn't the formal "your servant" either, which would have been proper if still more off-putting. What could Lucas wish of her that he insisted she wait in for him when he knew she'd a dozen errands to do for her mother's reception? And those silly endearments which he must have put in in case someone else read the note. Phillida shook her head. Well, if he were even half so up-in-his-altitudes as she suspected, she could get to her mantua makers for a fitting and home again long before he put foot out of bed.

Down in the housekeeper's room Flint, too, was reading a note: "If at all possible," it said, "delay Miss Morgan from leaving the house until Lord John has brought to her attention her danger." *Her* note was properly signed, "your servant, Z. Tuttles."

And how, wondered Flint, *am I to do that?* Flint thought and schemed and reluctantly decided to sacrifice Miss Morgan's least attractive walking dress. Early the next morning, her professional pride protesting all the way, Flint overheated an iron and, near the bottom, deliberately scorched the material. She made certain nothing else was ready to wear in that costume's place.

When Phillida rang for her, Flint delayed the morning routine as much as she could. She couldn't, however, drag out forever the dressing of a mistress who never fussed about her looks. She allowed Phillida to reach the front door before calling attention to the scorch mark. Her mistress suggested they ignore the problem, and it took all Flint's ingenuity to convince Phillida her pride would never recover if her charge were to appear in public that way. When she then "discovered" there was nothing else ready and something must be pressed, Phillida cocked her head and stared.

Flint flushed. "I'm sorry."

"About what are you sorry, Flint?"

Flint looked away, sighing. "Miss Morgan, when the accident happened yesterday, did it occur to you to wonder who tampered with the coach or to wonder why the coach was tampered with?"

Phillida grew very still. "Are you, too, suggesting it was to harm me?"

"Yes."

"So today you wish to make it impossible for me to go out?" Flint gripped her hands tightly and nodded. "And tomorrow? What about the next day? Am I ever to be free to come and go as I please?"

"I don't know. I was told to keep you in the house if at all possible until Lord John could speak with you."

"You were *told* . . ."

Flint's mouth compressed into a firm line. "Miss Morgan, do you believe I have your best interests at heart?"

"I thought so, but I begin to wonder. Did Lord John write you too?"

Flint's eyes widened. "You received a request from Lord John to wait for him and you intend to go out anyway?" She blushed. "I'm sorry. I've no business asking such an impertinent question. But I'm that worried I don't know if I'm on my head or my heels."

"But *why* are you so worried?"

"Someone wants to hurt you."

A vision of Lady John's face, the hatred burning in her eyes, flitted through Phillida's head. "But she's returned . . ."

Miss Morgan's gaze flipped to her maid's. Flint didn't pretend she'd not understood. "The lady in question left behind a servant who will stop at nothing when he has reason to do harm," she said quietly.

Phillida sat down rather suddenly in the slipper chair beside the window. "You appear to know more than I do. Tell me, Flint."

Flint, suppressing all references to the plots to bring Miss Morgan and Lord John together, explained her belief the servant had orders to harm Miss Morgan. "Before you scold me, I'll tell you straight out, I know what I've done, discussing you with my father and his friend, is wrong. But don't you see? I like you. I don't wish anything bad to happen to you."

"Flint, I can't like that you gossip about me with those men."

"No, miss. But if Mr. Tuttles hadn't told me about that evil man and then he hadn't told me about the carriage accident—which *you* didn't bother to mention—then how would I know you're in danger?"

"I can't quite put my finger on it, but I've a notion there is a hole in your logic. Or something you haven't told me?" she finished shrewdly.

Flint, wisely, said nothing. She waited to see if Miss Morgan would insist on going to her fitting. Just then a knock at the door brought both their heads around. Flint moved to it and accepted the salver on which a card lay, the corner tipped down. She carried it to Phillida.

"Hmm. Find me something to wear, Flint. Anything. We'll continue this interesting conversation another time. Beyond all expectation, Lord John has managed to arrive far earlier than I'd have believed possible."

A little later she opened the door to the parlor where

Rutgers had put her guest. She smiled at what she saw. Lord John might have managed to get up, but his head was not, she guessed, in the best of condition. She was halfway across the room before he lifted it from his hands and rose, carefully, to his feet.

"Sit down," she ordered softly. "You should not have forced yourself to come so early."

"Had to. Sir Clifford is still with his valet. I don't wish to go over this more than once, so may we wait?" he said only a trifle plaintively.

Phillida bit her lip. Had he come to break off the engagement? In spite of her better judgment, she'd taken heart from those unnecessary endearments in his note the night before, but why else would he be so serious this morning, so defensive? She made the resolution to face whatever was coming with fortitude. "We'll just sit here quietly so that you may suffer in peace."

"A woman of rare price. However did I get so lucky as to find you, my Lida?"

She relaxed an increment. That didn't sound as if he were wishing her to Jericho. Was he, too, fearful for her? Was that why he'd come?

It occurred to her to order coffee for the three of them. It arrived shortly before Sir Clifford. He, too, could judge when a man was not at his best and closed the door more softly than he otherwise might have done. His eyes twinkled as they met Phillida's. "Now, my lord, what may we do for you?" he asked, pitching his voice at a suitably low level.

Lord John was not quite so badly out of curl as they assumed. He was not so much hung over as in the dismals with worry. Now he straightened and looked into Sir Clifford's eyes. "You may help me convince Miss Morgan that we must be married immediately. She is in danger as long as she is my betrothed, Sir Clifford. I have had that brought forcibly to my attention."

Sir Clifford blinked. "In danger?"

"She didn't tell you of yesterday's accident?"

Phillida heaved a sigh. "It didn't seem particularly important, since no one was hurt."

"I see," said Sir Clifford after listening to Lord John's arguments, which included the interesting facts he'd been challenged by an honorable youngblood to a refereed fight at #13 Bond Street under Gentleman Jackson's careful eye—the winner to walk away with the other's seal—and that it had been necessary to thwart a pair of youngsters just down from Oxford who, in their cups, had had the brilliant notion they'd steal the seal. Sir Clifford crossed one leg over the other and narrowed his eyes, staring off at nothing in particular while he turned his lordship's suggestion over in his mind. "An immediate marriage would certainly reduce danger from idiots who have bet more than they can afford and might do you a mischief." He steepled his fingers. "However that may be, it seems to me, my lord, that Phillida might be even *more* endangered by your marriage—assuming your mother is the source of that danger," said Sir Clifford gently.

It was Lord John's turn to stare at nothing. There was a sad look about his eyes that made Phillida, sitting beside him on the confidant, lay her hand on the back of his. He turned his over and gripped hers tightly. But still he said nothing.

"Perhaps I go beyond the line," said Sir Clifford, "for mentioning her in such a context, but you yourself mentioned her groom . . ."

"However much I dislike the notion, I've been forced to consider my mother as a source of danger to Phillida. The groom is a bad lot. What's worse, he's disappeared. I don't *know* he caused the carriage accident, but it seems likely." He slumped back against the cushions.

"Sir Clifford, it feels so wrong to suspect her. My *mother*."

His arm went up and behind Phillida. The tips of his fingers rested on her shoulder. When she moved away, he changed position, too, regaining that faint contact. Phillida glanced at him, but he was looking at a point on the far wall, at nothing at all. Did he, she wondered, know he touched her?

Suddenly he seemed to return from wherever his thoughts had sent him. "Sir Clifford, I repeat: help me convince Phillida to marry me now at once. I can't protect her if I can't be with her. Married, we may go off on our wedding journey and be out of touch with the danger."

"You couldn't stay away forever."

"No. But"—a brief grin flashed across Lord John's face—"I envision a very long journey, and who knows what may have changed by the time we return?" He tipped his head; a hopeful look turned on Phillida encouraged the answer he wished.

Sir Clifford smiled, but the smile quickly faded. "You don't believe time alone will solve the problem. Nor could you be sure danger hasn't followed along behind you."

Lord John's hand dropped to Phillida's shoulder, tightened. "I believe I can protect her if only I have the right and the opportunity."

"It seems to me," said an agitated Phillida, rising to her feet and moving away from the upsetting touch, "that we are missing the simplest solution to the problem." She raised her head and stared at Lucas. "It is time," she said, "to stage the denouement of our little plan, my lord."

"There she goes, m'lording me again." Lord John sighed plaintively. "Sir Clifford, how do you convince a stubborn woman, who has taken a wrongheaded notion into her head, that things aren't what they seem, that you never had a desire to follow through with a plan which was never more than a brilliant ruse to allow one to get closer to the, er, other party involved?"

Sir Clifford grinned. "So. I was right. It was, originally, a sham engagement, was it not?"

Phillida swung away from the window through which she'd been staring. "You guessed?"

He nodded. "I've wondered if one or both of you wished things were different." He stared at his stepdaughter. She lifted her chin. "Phillida you must—"

"Stop. Not another word." Her breast heaved with growing agitation. "When we first discussed it," she said, "I warned Lucas he might be forced by circumstances into marrying me. Well, I won't be a party to it." She turned and glared at Lucas. "I will stage an end to this silly ploy of ours all by myself if *you* refuse to cooperate as we planned, my lord."

Lord John had automatically risen to his feet when Phillida did. Now he moved toward her, reached her, shook her lightly. "Damn you, woman, why won't you see that I *want* to marry you? Don't keep telling me I don't want what I *do* want. On the other hand"—his hands loosened, dropped—"if *you* don't wish to marry me . . ."

"You'll remember my views on that subject," she said, her head at a proud angle.

Sir Clifford harrumphed. "Phillida, dear, be careful." Her lips tightened and the chin rose another barely discernible notch. Her stepfather sighed and rose to his feet. "My lord, I can't advise you, but, given long experience of your beloved, I can tell you she becomes excessively stubborn once she takes a notion into her head. She's wrong so rarely that it takes a miracle to prove it to her when she is." He strolled toward the door. "I have yet to breakfast and am expected, shortly, at a meeting. Phillida, I will give orders to one of the footmen before I depart the house. He will be expected to accompany you whenever you go out and he will be let go without a character if he is left behind, *even if it is your doing*. You will go nowhere unprotected, do you hear me?"

"I am not foolish," said Phillida tightly. The hurt at her stepfather's lack of trust was aggravated rather than soothed by the fact, unacknowledged, that she'd already begun plotting ways of freeing herself from such escort.

"Phillida?"

She grinned, letting him see he'd won. "I'll be good."

"And *you,* my lord," Sir Clifford turned to Lord John. "You'd best find a way of convincing her of your change of heart before you lose her."

Lord John moved behind Phillida, his hands hovering over her shoulders. "I won't lose her—not if I have to carry her off by main force."

Sir Clifford looked thoughtfully from one to the other and nodded. Reprehensibly, he removed himself from the room and closed the door, leaving the pair alone. Lord John, expecting it, immediately clamped his hands down on her shoulders and turned Phillida into his embrace. He gave her no time to object, his kiss taking little account of her lack of experience. It took him a moment to realize she wasn't fighting him. He lifted his head and looked into her bemused face before picking her up and carrying her to the sofa. After seating himself with her lying across his lap, Lord John returned to the interesting occupation of convincing his love he loved her.

Phillida was much disheveled when he eventually attempted too much and frightened her with his ardor. She pulled away. "Lucas." His mouth returned to the sensitive area behind her ear and she twisted her neck against his mouth but, after a moment, she sighed. "Lucas, no."

"Hmmm."

"No more," she said sternly.

"More," he said, his hand once again moving away from her slim ankle and up under her skirt.

"No. Lucas stop."

He didn't release her, but he did sit back and look at her. It was his turn to sigh. "Thus endeth the lesson?"

Phillida felt heat in her neck and face. After one attempt to move away which he countered, she refused to struggle for her freedom. "I should never have allowed any of that, but I promised myself I'd know your kiss before we ended our charade. Well, now I know. And the charade is over. If you will not enact the farce we planned, then I will *pretend* you've done so. Our engagement is finished, my lord. I will send in the notice."

He grinned. "M'love, it won't work."

She ignored the endearment. "Of course it will."

"No. I didn't have *you* in mind when I gave the order, but there will be no more announcements in the papers. I've seen to that."

"I don't understand."

"The editors will print nothing which is unaccompanied by my seal. You are outgunned, my jewel. Our engagement will end conventionally. With our marriage," he added when she looked confused. "Lida, my dearest, I'm not trapped. I've not succumbed to chivalry. I'll not regret it once the knot is tied—Phillida," he added, holding her chin so she had to look him in the face, "I've fallen miles deep in love with you. And, despite your stubborn refusal to admit it, I believe you've fallen in love with me. That kiss, m'love, was no mere peck on the cheek. It is possible, of course, you were merely looking for adventure, but I don't think you're the sort to play such games. No," he concluded, shaking his head, "you love me and you'll marry me and," he sobered as he added, "together we'll end the danger in which I've inadvertently placed you. . . . Phillida?" he finished a trifle less firmly.

She stared at him. Her mind whirled. Could he mean it? Had he, too, found love where it was so unexpected? But why herself? "I'm such a nothing of a woman, Lucas. You've known such beauties. I'm not even blond! I don't understand how you *could* fall in love with me."

"I don't know *how* it happened, love"—he grinned and touched her cheek—"but I think, I know the *when*. It was the moment I discovered the second dimple. It only shows when you're up to some devilment, you know." He nodded solemnly. "I'd found a woman who will never bore me, and I'm no fool, my sweet: I decided right then to marry you." She didn't respond. His hands tightened, his head tipped to one side. "You *do* love me? *Don't* you?"

She swallowed, strain showing around her eyes. Dare she believe him? His fingers dug unconsciously into her sides. "Yes," she admitted. "Oh, yes. How could I not?"

"My love!" He held her close, his heart full to bursting. "It has been a case, '. . . when in sooth, substance seems shadow, shadow substance seems,'" he quoted.

"'When the broad, palpable, and marked partition, 'Twixt that which is and is not, seems dissolved,'" she finished.

They stared at each other, discovering at that odd moment another point in common: they both loved poetry! He pulled her close, his arms irresistible, his kisses intoxicating. But the couch was too short to accomplish all, and they were, rather rudely, brought back to a sense of propriety when they rolled to the floor.

"Good Lord, what have I done?" he asked, blinking down at her, holding himself away by an arm on either side of her.

"Very nearly seduced me?" she asked, both dimples appearing. "I think I'll marry you immediately, my lord.

Because if I don't, I'm not quite certain how I'll survive"— both dimples showed again—"and that survival has nothing to do with danger. I enjoyed the second lesson too much."

He touched her lips with his own. "Since you, too, feel that way, I suppose I can wait on events and then teach you the *third* lesson. We'll have a proper bed and time and needn't worry someone will knock, or, worse, open the door unexpectedly." He rose and helped her up. "Let me set you to rights, my dear." He'd just straightened her dress and pulled his coat into position when the door opened. Their eyes met, and they chortled.

"Well, how nice to see you both so gay," said Lady Rogers.

"Mother, we've decided to marry at once rather than wait until June."

"Have you? Sir Clifford thought you might."

"He did, did he?"

"Hmmm. I didn't understand it, quite, but he said something about a determined man could usually bring a practical woman to a sense of the necessity of, er, things?"

"This man was determined," said Lord John.

Phillida giggled. "And this woman definitely sees the necessity!"

Lady Rogers blinked. "Well, that's good. I think. We may announce it at the reception, may we not?"

"No." Lord John's hand closed around Phillida's shoulder, drawing her close. "That is, if Lida agrees to a quiet wedding, I wish us to marry and leave town with no one the wiser. At least, only our closest friends." He glanced from one woman to the other, wondering how he could justify such odd behavior since Lady Rogers had obviously not been told of her daughter's danger. "It's just that I detest all the nonsense a huge wedding requires. We'll have a notice placed in the papers after it is done. Phillida?"

"I have no desire for a large wedding."

"Oh, dear," said her mother. "You'll be cheating *me* of all the excitement. I've spent *years* planning for your wedding day . . . but it is your day, my dear . . . if you are certain you prefer something simple . . ."

"I very much prefer it, Mother. We must wait 'til after the reception, but, if my lord will purchase a special license, then I think we may be married by the end of the week."

"A whole week, love?"

She smiled a trifle shyly. "Will it be so very difficult?"

"Now I know what I'm missing?" he whispered into her ear, sending lovely shivers down her back. "My love, as yet you've no notion how difficult." But he could wait until the end of the week. A week? A week of danger he'd not be beside her to counter? "Phillida . . ."

"Hmmm?"

"You will be good, will you not?"

"Hmmmmmmm?"

"Lida!"

"Did you say something?"

"Not a thing," he said on a dry note. "Are you aware your mother has, most inexcusably, gone off and left us alone? Again?"

"I wondered when that would occur to you."

Lord John kissed first one and then the other dimple before beginning again with lesson two. The very important lesson, lesson three, he'd most reluctantly decided, must wait—no matter how difficult the waiting was.

The three conspirators grinned as three pewter mugs clinked. They drank.

" 'Twill be very nice, you joining our household, Missus Flint," said Tuttles.

"I look forward to it. Although your Lord John doesn't fit what my miss said was wanted."

"Nor is your Miss Morgan what Lord John wanted."

"No argufying!" said Porterman. "They *neither* knew what was wanted until they found it."

"I'll drink to that," said Tuttles, and did so.

Porterman sighed softly. "I wish I could believe we had anything to do with bringing them together, but I can't. Not really."

"I agree. Each thought to know what was wanted in a spouse, but Cupid was laughing all the while," said Flint.

"But there's still one thing, isn't there—the danger. What can we do about that?"

Flint shook her head. "I think we won't have much to do with solving that problem, either. Lord John will allow no one to harm my miss. He loves her."

Tuttles cleared his throat. "And does Miss Morgan love his lordship?"

Flint's eyes widened. "Of course she does. She's loved him forever."

"Then why did it take them so long to get things sorted?" asked Porterman.

"Why, because *Lord John* wouldn't admit *his* love for her, of course."

"He would have if your miss had only given him a hint!"

"My miss is a lady. She couldn't until he—"

"No more argufying." Porterman sighed. " 'Tis enough to make one think you two are married!"

There was an immediate silence. Tuttles cast a thoughtful look toward Flint. Flint blushed. And Porterman smiled into his ale.

Twelve

"That went rather well, don't you agree?" Lord John held his new wife around the waist, her back against him and his chin on her head. "Even your great-aunt, Lady Brookhaven, seemed to enjoy herself."

"She has found a rising star among the young Whigs and is enjoying herself to no end badgering her old friends in the party to do something for her protégé."

"So she no longer worries about Lord Brookhaven's politics?"

"Osbourn and she have made their peace. They've agreed to disagree, that is. I feared for a while she might disinherit him, and, although he has no real need for her fortune, I always hate to see relatives fall out to such a degree."

"I find I don't care much. I only care that I have you safe."

She tugged his arms more tightly around her and looked around the room where a few close friends celebrated the nuptials blessed only half an hour earlier by a kindly bishop, an elderly relative of Sir Clifford's. "Lucas, are you and Anthony *certain* your plan will work?"

"We've discussed it every way from Sunday."

She shuddered. "I can't help but worry."

"It can't possibly go awry."

"Hmmm."

"What does that mean?" he asked, nudging his chin into her scalp and tightening his arms around her.

"What if you don't capture the man?"

"We will."

"You're so certain."

A muscle in Lord John's jaw jumped. "M'love, I feel certain."

"I want to go. You'll be in danger."

"I must leave you here, because I'll not put *you* in danger."

"That isn't fair, is it?"

"Fair?" said her stepfather, coming up just then. "Phillida, it was one of the first things your father taught you, surely: life is rarely fair." He looked around and, lowering his voice, said, "I assume you are discussing the plan and are trying to talk yourself into a more active role."

"It *isn't* fair."

Lord John hugged her. "Phillida, love, don't you realize you'd be *adding* to my danger by coming along?"

She turned in her husband's arms and looked up at him. "Lucas?"

"If I must worry about you, m'love"—he touched her nose lightly—"I'll pay less attention to my own skin."

She sighed and laid her head against his heart. Over her curls Lord John winked at Sir Clifford, who quickly repressed a grin. It was Sir Clifford's opinion that his stepdaughter had met her match in more ways than one.

Lady Rogers scurried up. "I think, m'dear, it is time for you to change into your traveling clothes."

Phillida raised her head. Her eyes met her husband's and, for a long moment, they stared at each other. Once Phillida left the salon to go to her room, there was no telling how long before she'd see her beloved husband again—assuming she'd *ever* see him again. It *wasn't* fair. His lips thinned and his eyes narrowed in suspicion. She dipped her head. Oh, dear. *Could he read her mind?*

He pushed her chin up so he could look, again, into her eyes. His were steady, clear, and held a great deal of understanding. "Trust me?"

Lady Rogers sighed. "How romantic. Oh, my love, you have chosen a very dear man for a husband. Now come along. I'll just help you change." She gulped back a sob. "Oh, dear . . . my *baby*."

Phillida's eyes widened. Her gaze met Lucas's. They chortled. Phillida reached up to kiss him lightly. She tugged his head down so she could whisper in his ear. "I'll be good. I don't wish to endanger you, but don't you dare be long or you'll find yourself a widower for a different reason. I'll have worried myself into my grave."

"We'll come straight back. I don't wish to be long at this irritating bit of work, either. I've far more important things to do. With you."

Lady Rogers followed Phillida out of the room and was, in turn, followed by Sir Clifford. He stopped his wife, who showed signs, for the first time, of wishing him to the devil. He chuckled. "Love, let her go. She doesn't need your tears."

"But, Cliffie, I've not said a few words about . . ." She reddened. "Well, you know."

"I think you should leave that to Lord John."

"But . . ."

"Trust me?" Unconsciously he echoed Lord John.

"Well, what a question. Of course I do."

"Then don't follow Phillida." Lady Rogers frowned, and he pulled her into his embrace. "Did I," he asked solemnly, "tell you how much I love you?"

Her mood immediately lightened. "I can't," she said, tongue firmly in cheek, "at this very moment recall that you did."

"Then," he said, "it is an omission I'll correct just as soon we rid our home of all these totally unnecessary people."

"Hmm. I'll look forward to that."

"So," he said, solemnity lost in a grin which was only an instant away from a leer, "will *I*."

Half an hour later, those unnecessary people waved off the coach in which Phillida and her maid managed to be seated before anyone knew they'd left the house. Most guests left then, and the one or two remaining left soon after.

Phillida peeked out the window in her bedroom. A few minutes earlier she'd watched two smallish men, dressed in feminine clothing and pretending to be herself and Flint, tenderly handed into the coach by her new husband. Damn the man. He was *enjoying* the charade. She knew he was. She turned away and paced.

The door opened and Lady Rogers, stepping into the room, stopped short. "Phi—" The word was cut short by Flint, who, a hand against the older woman's mouth, moved her farther into the room and closed the door. "But you left. I watched you leave. Both of you. You were in the coach!" Bewilderment rang through every word. Phillida turned to go to her, her complexion white, her eyes blank. "Oh, my dear! My baby! What is it?"

Mother and daughter met in the center of the room. For a long moment Lady Rogers merely held her daughter. Then she said, "I think it is time you told me what has happened."

Phillida's eyes widened and her head tipped to a questioning angle. "But, Mother, do you mean *you don't know?*"

The door opened again and Sir Clifford stepped in, followed by Flint, who—with great stealth—had gone to fetch him. "It has come to my attention, m'dear," he said to his wife with something approaching asperity, "that you have stuck your delightfully retroussé nose into something of which you were to have known nothing."

"But . . ." Lady Rogers's eyes widened. "*You* knew? You *knew?*"

Sir Clifford looked quickly at Phillida, back to his wife. "You better clarify what you think I knew."

"My daughter. Her marriage. How could it fall to pieces so quickly?"

Phillida burst out laughing, the laughter turning to tears. "Oh, if only that were the case!"

"But . . ."

"Come, my dear. I'd best explain." Sir Clifford drew Lady Rogers to the satin-upholstered sofa at the end of Phillida's bed and seated her. "Now. Where to begin."

It was a rhetorical question, but Lady Rogers answered: "Why is my daughter *here* when she should be miles on her way to Dover, where she is to be taken aboard Lord John's yacht for the first part of her wedding journey?"

"She'll be on her way to Dover as soon as Lord John is prepared to return for her and, once again, set off on his wedding journey."

"But—"

"Actually," interrupted Phillida, "that isn't quite accurate. We're taking the villain to confront the villainess—assuming all goes well." She wrung her hands and turned back to the window across which Flint had pulled the drapes. Flint wouldn't allow her to open them even yet.

"I don't know, m'lady," said Flint, "that any who shouldn't is watching this window, but better no one know we aren't in that coach."

Phillida turned away. As she'd known, the waiting was unbearable.

"They'll be all right, Lida."

She stared painfully at her stepfather. "You can't know."

"Your Lucas and his friend were in the army. The runners who are pretending to be you and Mrs. Flint were handpicked. If the man makes an attempt on that coach, he will be captured."

"If he doesn't shoot first and from ambush and never come near it." Her voice rose with each word, her fear pushing it to something close to a shriek.

"Hush now! Phillida, I don't believe he can do it that way."

"Why?" Phillida's eyes were huge in a tightly drawn face.

"Because he can take no chances on missing. He's not a trained shot, Phillida. I asked about that. It's possible he's done a bit of poaching in his time, but, if so, it was of the snare-setting sort. You must not imagine horrors, m'dear."

Phillida slid down to the floor, putting her head in her mother's lap and her arms around her waist. Over her head Lady Rogers looked helplessly at her husband, her hands busily soothing her daughter. Even in her misery Phillida was aware of the oddness of the situation. It had, in the past, always been herself who soothed her mother. She lifted her head and met older eyes. "Thank you," was all she said, but both knew something had changed between them.

"Have you a guess, sir, where the villain will strike?" asked a deep voice, which sounded odd coming from the heavily veiled person dressed in the neat gray gown of a superior abigail.

"We think it will be where he expected his contrived carriage accident to happen. Our suspicion is that once before he waited there, in vain, to pounce. It's a nasty hill with a sharp turn partway up. The horses will be laboring, and the driver will slow still more to make the turn."

"Hmm. I remember that corner, I do," said an even deeper voice from the less soberly dressed feminine figure on the seat beside Lucas. "Belike it'll come about there, as you say, m'lord."

There was a placidity in the tone that required a pipe, and, to make conversation, Lord John asked if the runner smoked one.

"I don't know how you guessed, m'lord, but, aye. And I'm missing the old black bowl about now!"

"It was good of the two of you to masquerade as women," said Lord John. "Do you find it necessary to do this sort of thing very often?"

"Nawr. Never before." The man pretending to be Phillida shifted and, after Lord John had assumed he was done speaking, added, "Right uncomfortable it is, too. Didn't know ladies had to wear suchlike. Poor dears."

The fit of loquaciousness lapsed, and Lord John, thinking of nothing more to say, turned to look out his window. They were approaching the hill, and the sort of tension he'd not felt since the Peninsula began to evidence itself in him. For half a moment it registered that, for a very long time now, he'd neither thought about, nor been in the mopes about, his years as a soldier. Which was another thing for which he could bless Phillida. The poor dear would be in a fret about him. Poor dear indeed, he thought, a smile playing about his lips, but his eyes were alert to any oddity in the landscape. Either it would happen soon or he was wrong and the next few weeks would be hell, as he had to be constantly on the alert for danger.

"Should be about there, sir," said one runner, his tension palpable.

"Yes. You both know your role in this?"

"Yezzir. We don't expect but the one man. The guard riding in the boot will be careful before he shows himself." A shot rang out. "Well, sir, you'll be pleased to know your guess was correct." There was a great deal of satisfaction in the runner's voice.

The coach pulled up. Voices could be heard arguing. Then the devil they'd come to meet had them out of the carriage and standing in a row. A wildness in his eyes, the dowager's groom controlled his mount with one hand while a gun wavered between Lord John and the sham Lady John. When the disguised runner reached up and lifted off the hat and veil, the gun jerked to a steady aim.

"Sorry to disappoint you," said Lord John quietly, "but I couldn't allow you to harm my wife."

The gun shifted back to him, and they could see sweat running down the side of the groom's face.

"You'd best give up now."

"Damn you . . ."

"If you shoot, my mother will never forgive you," said Lord John just as gently—but his seeming calm hid a pounding heart. Why didn't the third runner get into place and finish it? The groom was nervous, and nervous men were dangerous, unpredictable. Lord John wasn't particularly afraid of being shot—not that he'd ever enjoyed the pain, but he wanted very much to return to Phillida. To be laid up with a wound which might be long in healing didn't fit in with his plans. Not at all. *Ah,* he thought, seeing a movement behind their villain. Now to distract the groom long enough so the runner could pull him from his horse and capture him. "I don't believe you wish to upset my mother, do you?"

The groom didn't reply.

"She did you a rather large favor when she saved you, the last time you were in trouble—from transportation, if not worse. Do lay down that popper and we'll go see m'mother and get this settled."

The gun wavered again but then steadied, this time pointed at the second female figure. That runner, rather quickly, raised his hands and removed his hat. An indescribable sound escaped the groom's throat. Suddenly he turned the gun and pressed it to his chest. Instantly two things happened. The gun went off and the groom was pulled from his horse into the arms of the third runner, who had finally managed to get close enough to reach him.

"Is he dead?" asked Lord John.

"Just a shoulder wound. My pulling at him spoiled his aim. He'll do."

"I suppose we must find a leech and have that bullet removed." Lord John thought of still more time wasted. Phillida would never forgive him. He looked at the villain's horse and, not completely surprised, recognized one of his own. He grinned. "Tony, old friend," he said as the "coachman" strolled over, "I've another little job for you if you're agreeable."

"I saw you eyeing the horse. Go on with you and reassure your bride. Can't say I blame you. We'll be along when we've patched him up." He turned a thumb toward where the shorter of the two runners was applying a bandage to the groom's oozing shoulder.

"I dislike leaving you with this mess."

"But you dislike still more leaving your lady in suspense an instant longer than necessary, so *move*."

"Yes, sir," said Lord John with a grin and a mock salute. "I'm off."

* * *

"Phillida, love," said Sir Clifford, "you will make yourself ill."

"I should have gone with him. I should be there. That man is evil. He'll kill everyone. I'll never see Lucas again."

"Stop it." Lady Rogers slapped her only offspring sharply across the face. "Stop it this instant." Phillida, shocked, ceased rocking back and forth. The moaning stopped. "Now, you are an adult woman of reasonable intelligence. You will, at once, begin acting like one."

Phillida drew in a deep breath, sobbed once, and, realizing what her mother had done, blinked. She turned surprised eyes on Sir Clifford.

"I told you your mother was a capable woman when allowed the chance to be so," said her stepfather with a soft chuckle.

"I can remember thinking," said Phillida, "that I was glad you'd married Mother because if you hadn't then I wouldn't have felt free to marry Lucas." She blushed. "How could I have been so wrong?"

"Your father *wanted* your mother to be a widgeon, because that made him feel much more the proper man, you see."

"My father," said Phillida, a dangerous note in her voice, "was the most intelligent man I've ever met."

"Yes," agreed Sir Clifford, "he was when it came to his books and his writing. But he was hopelessly incapable of running his day-to-day life. How old were you when you took over the accounts?"

Phillida's eyes widened. She blinked. Had her father, whom she'd admired, been so . . . one-sided?

"I didn't mind so very much," said her mother, "except when he wished you to be raised with as few feminine skills as possible. He wanted a son so badly, you know."

"I didn't know. I hated the lessons you made me learn." Phillida smiled reminiscently. "Having spent hours learning my Latin and maths, I thought it unfair I then had to turn to music and embroidery. Especially since Father pooh-poohed the necessity."

"It *was* necessary, m'love." Lady Rogers smiled at her husband. "Do you suppose we might have some tea to pass the time?"

Phillida interjected, "I think you and Sir Clifford should go do something else. How can you explain being in this room for so long?"

"I have a feeling we've already given all that away. Either it is all right or it is already too late. We shall all adjourn to the salon and order tea."

Phillida was slowly finishing her third cup when the sound of the rapid approach of a horse drew her to the window. This time no one stopped her when she flung back the drapery and threw open the window. She leaned out.

"Lucas!"

He looked up and grinned at her. "All's bowman, m'love—as my new acquaintances would say."

"Does that mean you caught the man?"

"We did. Let me come in and I'll tell you all about it." He tossed his reins to a raggedly dressed boy loitering in the street and ran up the steps to pound on the front door.

Rutgers, slow to respond, opened it. He gaped. "Lord John? But you . . ." Rutgers craned his neck, but there was no sign of the new Lady John. So, thought the butler with satisfaction. Obviously, his lordship had strangled the wench already. The sound of running feet on the stairs made the butler turn to see who was rushing down at such a breakneck speed. His jaw dropped.

Lord John set the butler aside and was barely prepared for the onslaught when Phillida threw herself at him. Their kiss was deep and desperate. "Worried about me, love?" he asked when he finally raised his head. His hand brushed back her hair. "I thought you said you'd trust me."

"He could have shot you from ambush. You might have had no chance."

"In the end he tried to kill himself, but he couldn't even do that right. We'll have the runner's help when we take him to confront . . ." He looked at the butler and suggested they adjourn to the salon. A little later he'd finished describing the capture and continued, "Now I know she meant you harm, Lida, I'll have her escorted to a ship which will take her to her brother in the West Indies."

"And the man?"

"He'll be transported, love."

"Won't your mother wish him to go with her?"

"As a constant reminder of *why* she's in exile? I think not." He kissed her again. "I wish we needn't postpone our leave-taking yet again."

"Does her perfidy hurt very badly?"

"Surprisingly little. I admit I've felt guilty most of my life that I can't love her as one should love one's mother. But she's never allowed it. It has always been as if I were a necessary duty, one she rather loathed, but fulfilled to the best of her ability."

Phillida hugged him, lay her head on his shoulder. "How could any woman feel that way about her own son?"

"I don't know, Lida love. Do you think your mother would mind our staying here tonight? The fewer people to know we're still in town, the better. Which reminds me that I must have a word with that butler."

"I already have. With all the servants." Sir Clifford chuckled. "They are quite confused."

Sometime later, Major Ayers arrived. Once he'd greeted his host, the major turned to Lord John. "All's bowman," he said, "as our new acquaintances would say." He never did understand why Lord and Lady John doubled over laughing.

The next day Lord and Lady John's coach was followed by a carriage containing the runners and the groom. Major Ayers rode, declining to join the lovers in their coach. Once they arrived, the confrontation was not a particularly peaceful one, the groom insisting he'd not go to the gallows alone and the dowager Lady John equally insistent she'd never ordered that anyone be hurt, that the groom had gone far beyond what had been asked of him which was nothing more than a mere prank. Or so she swore. Everyone pretended to believe her, but even she was aware that no one did. Her dignity intact, she went to her room where she took her temper out on her maid who promptly gave notice.

"That was awful," said Phillida a little later. "I feel terrible."

"I never knew she hated me," mused Lucas, shaken by the interview which had meandered off into other areas as such interviews tend to do.

"She loves power. She craves it, I think," said the major, sipping the brandy handed him by the aged family butler.

Lucas nodded. "This time she went too far—although I truly think the groom overstepped orders which did not include anyone's death."

"You're certain she's resigned to going to her brother?" asked Phillida.

"Yes. She's agreed that a pleasant sea voyage and a

long stay in the West Indies would be just the thing. You see, she's finished in England. She knows I'll not allow her perfidy to pass with no notice. While she oversees her packing, I'll write a letter that the captain of the ship on which she'll sail is to give her to her brother."

"Luke, you aren't forgetting legal arrangements must be made about her jointure and that sort of thing are you?"

"Such arrangements can be completed at a later date. I want her gone as soon as may be."

"She can't go alone with no female companionship, and her maid has given notice, you know," said Phillida. "Can you pay someone to go with her on board ship, Lucas? What if she must endure *mal de mer,* for instance?"

"Is there no end to it? Blast it, when may we begin our marriage trip?"

"Why don't you go? I'd enjoy supervising the dowager's leave-taking." Major Ayers grinned a rather wolfish grin. "What's more I can think of just the companion for her. One wouldn't have to pay her the earth; nor is she the sort to be bamboozled by her ladyship. In fact, she's quite the lady herself these days and will enjoy putting one over on your mother! You see, she's getting a little old for the trade she now plies and has been looking for a new career."

"You can't mean she's the sort I think you mean, can you?" asked Phillida, half horror struck and half amused.

"Now what sort would that be?" The major's grin widened. "She's a big woman, Phillida, and won't take any nonsense. She'll talk what she calls flash as long as Lady John behaves—but Lady John will soon understand she can't bully Dolly." He chuckled. "Dolly was good to me when I was green behind the ears, Luke. I think I can do her a good turn: with a small nest egg, she'll do well in the Indies." He waggled his eyebrows suggestively. "If she hasn't enough saved, I'll give her what she'll need to set up a house of the sort she'd like to run. Call it a wedding present!"

"If you truly don't mind doing that for us," said Lucas, "why are we lounging around here? I've a yacht awaiting us in Dover, Lida love . . . and more I wish to teach you," he added softly.

She flushed, deeply embarrassed despite last night's long hours in bed with her husband. She glanced sideways at her husband's friend who stared into the empty grate pretending he'd not heard Lucas's comment. "I'll ask Flint to pack up the little she unpacked," said Phillida, just a trifle on her dignity, and exited the room, rapidly regaining her equilibrium.

"That," chided Ayers, "was uncalled for, putting her to the blush that way."

Lucas was unrepentant. "She better get used to it. At least until I can, with some hope of success, learn to restrain my urge to take her to bed."

Phillida walked back into the room as he finished speaking and, her temper ruffled, forgot she'd come to ask if Flint should also pack for him. Hmm, she thought. So *she'd* better get used to it, had she? Both her dimples came into evidence. "Lucas," she said sweetly, satisfied when his head swung around to stare at her. "Haven't you forgotten something?"

"What?" he asked cautiously, his eyes flitting toward the major and back, warily, to his wife.

"Unlike you, I'm very new at the games you're teaching me. I think it may take me *much* longer to learn restraint than it will you." She batted her eyelashes at him before exiting with a flirt of her skirts.

Silence reigned for all of ten seconds. Then Major Ayers burst into laughter. "I never thought to see *you* red around the gills, Lucas." He chuckled and raised his glass to the doorway through which Phillida had disappeared. "I think you've truly met your match, ol' friend."

It wasn't, however, a match made in Heaven. Exactly. The imp in Phillida took her apprenticeship to the devil in Lucas very seriously indeed, and there was soon— according to their long-suffering friends—not a ha'porth of difference to be found between them.